Stories We Tell

Stories We Tell

S. A. Mills

Published 2013 by Shorehouse Books
Printed in the United States of America

ISBN 0-615-91990-1
EAN-13 978-061591990-4

This story is entirely fictional. Any similarities to real people, places, or events were entirely unintentional.

Special Thanks

Roxanne Nawrot

Sylvia Nawrot

Donna Cavanagh

A.K. Cholewinski

Celine Kniep

Ed Cavanagh

Sue Johnson

Talyor Corso

Justina Ellis

Lacy Ruffalo

Kym Lafever

Margaret Andrews

I would like to dedicate this book to my children as well as to my grandson and any future grandchildren that may come along to bless my life. This is your legacy in more ways than one. I love each of you more than words can say.

And I owe a debt of gratitude to the times and the culture that I was blessed to grow up in. For the words contained herein are all drawn from the gentle voices and the gentle stories that were whispered amongst a dying breed of individuals. And it is to them that I owe the most gratitude.

This fragile time, fragile place and truly gentle people who are best memorialized as follows...

Forgotten

Harps and fiddles and dirt roads that ran parallel with streets of gold were the dreams that shook hands with the often-harsh realities during the birth of the new south. The birth was a fragile one; no more than a few decades in length. A small, almost forgotten era when the outhouses and one-room school houses the people knew so well were unbeknownst to them teetering on a rim of obscurities too numerous for their comprehension. New and changing ways were merely distant echoes coming from up North somewhere. To them, they were not very likely to invade the harsh way of life they knew as well as the rich soil of their farms.

Their families were large, often numbering ten or more children, out of necessity, as much as the loving desires of the married folk. There was a certain strength in numbers-- a strength in love. It seemed that the higher the numbers, the stronger the bonds of love.

I'm speaking of a time when the ways and ideas of 1840 were the advice and stronghold of day to day life throughout the 1940s. I'm speaking of a place, of many hidden places, where pockets of rich farmlands that made up communities were somehow frozen in time—times that were so long passed yet a day's horse ride from the times we'd all recognize as the 1930s and 1940s.

I'm speaking of communities—communities where no one who had a dozen children spilling out of a four- room house was poor. These were places where the depression hadn't hit hard because hard times like hard work had been the people's legacy. Hidden coves of times when women, despite their many back-breaking duties, still grew their hair long because it was their glory and a man's mule was his livelihood. Places where a helping hand was a way of life and respect was an unwritten law that everyone was careful to observe; a community that came together to replace what was lost to a neighbor. The men would appear with the materials they had on hand and the womenfolk without the benefit of phones and despite miles of isolation from one another, would know, as if by instinct, what to bring in addition to a few housekeeping-start-up essentials, in order to lay a feast before those hard-working men.

And after the work and the food and a prayer for the safety and prosperity of the community, someone would bring out a fiddle, another a guitar, and music would fill the air. Yes, within these hidden coves lay an insurance that no modern company could ever provide. For their insurance was an assurance that came from a way of life the Good Book prescribed.

The Good Book was at the center of every social event these communities knew. From the spring homecomings at the small white clapboard church where the joyful strands of Rock Of Ages quietly gave way to long-winded sermons of how Christ is the rock for all ages, which gave way to a feast of

Mrs. Johnson's fried chicken and Mrs. Steward's green beans and Grandma Jones' fried apple pies served outside the church from tables made of planks laid over sawhorses, and eaten off real plates while seated on old quilts spread upon the ground. These dinners were followed by more hymns of praise, a few more words from the preacher and someone giving their soul to Jesus.

The heat and hard work of summer gave way to seven nights of revival at that old church. For seven nights, work was ended early and supper was eaten early. The hot tired members of the community gathered with the women and children sitting inside on the hard slat benches waiting and praying for a cool evening breeze to float through the raised windows all the while fanning themselves with homemade cardboard fans glued onto giant popsicle sticks. Their gaze often looked upward when the familiar buzz-tap sound of a wasp was heard over the out-of-tune piano or the visiting preacher's words.

The menfolk stood outside the open doors and windows listening and talking in whispers of this year's crops and weather as they whittled and carved pieces of cedar being careful to bow their heads in reverent silence whenever a prayer was said.

The fall, with all its harvest and preparation for winter, included canning the vegetables, patching the roofs, collecting the hay, replacing and repairing quilts, and laying in the firewood. It also meant

Brush Arbor meetings. Held out of doors in some clearing with lanterns hanging from trees, the ladies and small children sat on splintered boards, as hymns without that old out-of-tune piano were offered up from memory by all, even by the menfolk who stood around the back of the meeting area. These were the true revivals, for the hearts and minds of all present were serious. Perhaps, because the winter's nip in the morning air signaled the end of not just another crop season but the end of yet another season in everyone's life. And as the page was turned silently in their lives, many lives were rededicated and returned to Christ, the author and finisher of their fate.

Glimpses of this forgotten era, a forgotten way of life are all I had--brief, faint glimpses yet I was blessed. Blessed by the cool freshly drawn well water drank from a home-grown, hand-carved gourd dipper. The smell of thousands of meals that permeated the old hand hewn, three-room home still fill my senses, blessing me, even now as they bring my soul and my memories together as one.

There are afternoons when I feel that even that old outhouse just down the path blessed me. Even now memories of the forever breezes that swept across that old front porch cool me on a hot summer's day when I close my eyes and go back to that time and that place where I knew a love and acceptance that went beyond obligation.

Most of all I was blessed by the gentle graces of a great-grandmother who taught me to listen to the trees talk and who loved to remember, who loved to love, and who made one and all of her ever expanding brood feel welcomed, accepted, and wanted.

The stories that come together in this book forming one tale are dedicated to the rich southern voices, of my paternal Great-grandmother Verda Mae Robinson Finley; my maternal Grandmother Sabra Dimple England Howard; my paternal Grandfather Woodley Ralph Farley and my Grandmother Reba Jewel Finley Farley. It is their memories, adages, legends, and lives from which all the stories in this book are drawn and formed as one story just as they formed the subtle legacy that is a large part of my family tree.

So, it is to them that I gratefully dedicate this work. For without their love and the powerful influence they had in my life, none of these words would have been possible.

On behalf of Verda, Sabra, Woodley, Reba and myself we'd like to welcome you to come in, sit back and enjoy the memories, as well as the legends that formed and continue to form our lives.

Houses

They are scattered all over middle Tennessee. Some of them sit right alongside obscure one-lane dirt roads; others dot the sides of the interstate, left years ago, alone and abandoned to the elements with their tin roofs fading to rust and unpainted doors turning black in their shameful rot. Glassless windows staring out like vacant black eyes, somehow sinister, yet very sad; they sit on in watch, a silent witness to times long past and the new times marching on.

Sometimes, you'll find a newly planted cornfield parting its straight rows briefly for a forgotten home to continue on in its lonely existence. The walls that once played host to families now play host to farm tools, hay and fertilizers. Yet the house stands on, enduring come what may as if in hope.

You'll find these houses in the middle of cow pastures. They are sprawling two-story colonials, their southern charm and grace hang on about them as veils of tears. Their once prideful columns seem to sag in lonely disgrace. The now faded but once finely papered walls, that at one time played host to that famous southern hospitality, now echo their memories to the parties of field mice and wayward raccoons.

Trampling through the woods miles from the nearest road, you'll run upon four walls who witnessed the roofs fall in silent neglect cursing themselves for somehow not being strong enough to endure. In the stillness--if you listen hard enough--you can almost hear the distant chatter of the family that left behind the rotting wooden bucket over there by that fieldstone well or the ladder back chair that balances just so on the rotting, sagging porch.

Sometimes, what is left forgotten is not a house but a building or perhaps a barn or an old gristmill or maybe what once was a church or school.

Yet, no matter what their titles once were, they remain scattered all over middle Tennessee; these houses, these buildings, stand on in forgotten infamy, defying the laws of nature and neglect. Here and there foundations remain, left as untouched as the houses they once supported. Most bear witness to a brave vandal's fire. Unbeknownst to them, the vandals had the powers that held those buildings together, bringing the punishment of life long suffering to them for their crimes. Their crimes against the ultimate force of a nature not yet explored.

It is not neglect that holds stone and mortar or board and nail together for fifty to a hundred years without repair. It is not sacred memories, for often times these lands are quite valuable and change hands in ownership; yet, new owners seem to let these buildings stand on.

Their continued existence can be explained by what was brought into these homes all those many years ago. What allows these forgotten manmade edifices to stand unthreatened, when logic and even science said they should have fallen, is energy. The energy of tired, prejudiced, angry feelings – ushered in by desperate angry people. People, who all too often made bargains with the wrong entities, or whose envious, grievous, heinous thoughts and actions, left the imprints of energy like cement in the walls. Sometimes, it was crimes of passion and hate that created an energy that held on to the future by clinging to the worse moments of the past.

These unspeakable thoughts and acts of family members one and all seem to adhere themselves to the walls growing stronger with each new family that comes until finally their doors and windows are shut for all time. Yet through time they wait often permeating the ground so that any new building will be able to serve as a new home for the energy forces that were once these houses.

For those who walk in darkness, these places hold a must-enter fascination, a sick sort of welcome. For those who walk in light, these places offer up feelings of sadness and foreboding. For those who walk in the knowing light these houses hold an evitable feeling, a need for healing.

These places stand scattered not just in Tennessee but throughout the United States, and the world. The hate, anger, and envy that gave these places their stabs at immortality are the very cornerstones of evil; an evil that can last and grow laughing in the face of all the odds, of all the beliefs. Perhaps it is because of the beliefs that people forget their roots and in doing so, fall victim.

For those of us who know things past all reason, we cannot forget, because we know that forgetting our history, forgetting our legacy will only serve the forces behind the scenes acting as a gateway for us to relive that history and reinforce that legacy.

It is a house that lies behind my family's legacy. It is a house and its energy that sat vacant scaring all others away for decades just as it drew me close in. And it is a house, that one house, which is at the center of the stories I will tell here in these pages. And in order to tell the one story I have to tell it in multiple stories ,so that not one insight not one nuance is lost that work together to form the legend and the legacy.

To begin to understand the house and its power one must first come to understand the family, my family, which gave birth to the energy that surrounded this house, my birthright. And to come to know and understand the terror that faced me as I fought the good fight one must first come to know what happened to my uncle and his family, my family, as their own power grew. In so doing, you will come to understand just how a building meant to be a home can come into a power all its own. For this sort of power starts with one person, one thought, one set of unjust desires. And each person starts with a family of persons who sire and persons who raise and nurture; persons who in all their well meaning often leave a lacking that grows in the one they love.

I now open the door to this flawed family of mine, to this sad legacy, to the very home at its center and ask that only the brave of heart and the pure of spirit turn the pages as I share my bitter legacy as well as all its cherished gifts that were born of this legacy.

Sisters

It was 1895 in Spirit Springs, Cedars County, Tennessee. But it could have been 1865 or1800, for nothing had changed much in almost a hundred years. Though well south of the Mason Dixon Line, not one son or father in this hidden hamlet, some fifty or sixty miles from the nearest rail line, had fought in the Civil War; there was nothing at stake for these hard working people, at least to their way of thinking. With the exception of a hand full of the town's more traveled residents, no one in Spirit Springs had ever seen a person of color much less owned one.

The idea of slavery was just a little impractical amongst these honest God-fearing people. Feeding their children and livestock was a struggle, just how would one go on to feed and clothe a slave? Of course the initial cost was another matter all together in this community where barter, not silver or gold, was the primary source of currency.

Those considered wealthy were the ones who had a lot of livestock and land. One of the largest landowners in Spirit Springs was a man known as John Sedler. John was married to a woman called Martha, and they were no ordinary couple.

John, who would eventually father four children, was a quietly gifted man. He was not considered gifted because of his remarkable woodworking abilities, or carpentry skills, and it wasn't just his ability to grow the finest crops or breed the finest livestock. John was considered gifted because he could move objects with his mind, start and stop fires the same way and these were givens that the whole community knew about. What they didn't know was that he could read their minds and see into their very souls.

What the community depended on was John's gift for divining, the art of finding water. Not only could he tell where the water could be found, but he also knew just how deep to dig, and just what the quality and quantity of the water would be.

And perhaps it was because of this ability that John offered to anyone--free of charge--that he had been allowed to live in peace in this often times backward, always God-fearing and superstitious community.

John's wife Martha was also gifted. She was known far and wide as a healer, and was often called upon to save valuable livestock, and though her success rate with humans was not quite as good, due to the distrustful nature of humans, she had been credited with saving more than a few lives and helping to birth more than her fair share of the children that were born to this community.

John accepted his wife's gift and allowed that it was because of her gift that he could not read her thoughts--only her emotions. If he could have seen inside her, he would have known that she could foresee the future and that just by touching an object, she could see its past.

What neither of them understood about their gifts was that a truly gifted person cannot read another truly gifted person's thoughts. Maybe at that time it was best that they didn't fully understand the gift and its rules. Truth is that very little was known of the gift or its powers then.

In the late spring, June the 6th to be exact of 1895, Martha gave birth to twin girls Amelia and Cecilia, both born with veils, a gauzy film that covered their eyes. It was carefully noted in Martha's Bible that Amelia's was pink in color and almost as thick as silk, while Cecilia's was a very thin, almost a transparent white.

Now John knew that the veils meant that his daughters were gifted, yet he was still sorely disappointed by their birth. His disappointment lay not just in the fact that his firstborn were girls and girls were by all accounts considered weak, but lay with his God who had promised him a son--a son who would be gifted with a sight far beyond his own. Already he'd been instructed in exactly the way in which to raise this boy.

The evening of his daughters' births, John took his feelings of betrayal and went out deep into the woods behind his home. There he built an altar and prayed to the only God he knew and understood. He bartered with this God, for his God was a bartering God. He returned to the house two days later a changed man, accepting and celebrating the birth of his daughters.

Over the next ten months, the girls grew and developed perhaps a little ahead of their ages, perhaps not. For they grew in a time when there were no growth and development charts, no pressure. A baby was a baby until it could walk and talk, then it was considered a child capable of learning tasks and doing chores. Each additional birthday meant an additional chore or two until the child reached fourteen or fifteen and was thusly trained and capable of marrying and establishing and running a home of their own.

Early on Amelia established herself as a demanding child; she cried often and loudly. Displaying quite a mean-spirited temperament by the time she could crawl and sit up around the age of ten months. She was a large-framed child with chubby yet surprisingly nimble fingers that picked up everything in her path. She was the feminine duplicate of her father with a shockingly thick black head of hair that showed body but no hint of curls.

Cecilia was a direct contrast of her sister in every way. She was a quiet and happy baby, bubbling over with smiles and pleasant coos, delighting all that came in touch with her. She began to crawl a month later than her sister, and very rarely displayed any sense of a temper; she always seemed to her mother to be in a quiet, contemplative thought. Where Amelia was large and stocky with an olive complexion, Cecelia was small-boned and delicate with the complexion of a porcelain doll. Her hair and eyes were as her mother, auburnwith her delicate face framed in curls.

It was the end of April 1896, an unseasonably warm day, and the twins sat facing one another on the back porch. As John came up the path that led from the barn, he stopped and watched as the girls, laughing in delight, manipulated small stones in the air between them. At that point, he felt himself bursting with pride as he realized just how much of him they had coursing through their veins. From that day forward he set aside at least three hours to spend with the girls, one per each and one for both. Thus he began their education just as his father had begun his education.

Martha had watched the same scene from her kitchen window, unlike her husband who was filled with pride by the event, she was filled with dread. From that day forward she set aside specialized time for her daughters as well, and doted more heavily on Cecelia.

Over the next four years, John saw the girls develop powers that showed great promise. It did bother him that Cecelia showed a gift toward healing, for that was one extra gift that Amelia did not have. It was at this point that he expressed a definite preference toward Amelia.

By the time Amelia was three she had made herself her father's shadow, which was a great relief to Martha. For no matter how hard she tried to tell herself she was being foolish, each day found her more and more repulsed by the feeling of evil that came over her each time she held Amelia to her.

Cecelia, however, was a ray of hope to her. While John and Amelia were off and about, Martha trained her daughter in the art of reading tea leaves, coffee grounds, clouds and the signs and omens found in nature. She and Cecelia also took walks where she taught her daughter about the roots and leaves used in the art of healing, as well as lessons in levitations, mind reading, and finding the past in objects and people. And very quietly, as a secret, she taught her daughter of her God and the redemptive and loving powers that she believed could be found in the blood of Jesus.

The girls' schooling was briefly interrupted in August of 1900 by the birth of Haas Longmoore Sedler. John's promised son entered the world feet first almost killing his mother and weighing in at ten pounds. He was a strong and healthy baby boy with the looks of his father, and he was born with a thick, almost transparent in color, veil over his face.

John was delighted beyond even his own belief by the appearance of this child and looked forward to the day when the boy would show signs that he was ready to begin his training. Unlike with his daughters, John would have to wait two long years.

Two very important years if you believe that the first seven consecutive years of life are the most important for anyone with the gift. For it is very important for the knowledge to be imparted early in life and without interruption, for so much is lost with age and maturity. One becomes less trusting of his or her senses overtime especially when those students start to meet with the outside world. Yet it is by the same token and understood that education cannot begin until the child shows a definite ability.

Early on, Amelia sensed an importance about Haas and jealousy filled her. From violent tantrums directed at Martha, whom she considered responsible for the existence of Haas, to running away and losing herself in the woods for one and two days at a stretch. She did everything her young mind could conceive of to divert her father's attention away from Hass and onto her. Finally at the age of six she settled on hard work at her gift as the perfect way to gain his attention. And over the next two years, she developed her abilities at what to Martha was an alarming rate.

While Amelia was busy being Amelia, her twin, (and it was about this time that the idea of the two being twins was getting hard to grasp), Cecelia became very close to her mother. She helped to care for Haas, as she too was working and learning her gift. Her mother was teaching her that good must overcome evil and that walking in light was powerful, for dark could not overcome true light, but true light could send darkness away. She learned that goodness was peace and that an evil person could never truly know the feelings of peace. Unbeknownst to everyone else, except herself, Martha was trying to undo a most certain destiny.

Slowly the days blended into weeks, the weeks faded into years, and Haas had begun his father's training after his mother's well-spent first two years. Amelia became more of a loner spending greater spans of time in the woods finding various plants and herbs, Martha teaching her their names and uses. To Amelia, Martha was only serving a purpose. The only person other than her father that Amelia spoke to was her sister. Cecelia's earnest goodness was a source of unexplainable delight to her.

Fate, being what it is, stepped in and allowed destiny to correct its course, and when Haas was seven and the twins were twelve, Martha delivered her last child, a daughter, Bessie Marie.

The new infant was barely five pounds and entered the world with such a thin transparent veil that she was scarcely noticed by her father at all. But Martha, now weaker with age and the strains of childbirth, took great delights in the little girl with the auburn ringlets and midnight blue eyes. This child all but ignored by her father, who had his hands full with Amelia and Haas, would become her mother's saving grace.

Surprisingly, Amelia was not at all affected by the birth of Bessie Marie as both John and Martha had feared. Perhaps it was because she was older or maybe it was because she had too much else on her mind. The next four years passed peaceably with Haas maturing, learning and developing. The only problem John saw with Haas was that he had what John felt was an unnaturally deep affection for his mother. Thus her influence, though very small in his training, was noticeable.

Now don't get me wrong, John loved Martha. He loved her with a vengeance. It's just that good attracts evil, light attracts dark, like flies to honey, and while John was not evil per say, he was dark. Martha was pure light. And I think that we all know that one must eclipse the other. John considered the gift just that-- a gift. While Martha, whom I believe was surely more truly gifted than John, looked upon the gift as more of a curse. In time John picked up on her feelings and they grew apart. Having met in that place where light and dark always do, at dawn; they'd stay apart until the sunset of their years together, which would come sooner than either would know.

When the twins turned sixteen, troubles struck the Sedler house and a battle of powers brewed. And though I had not yet been born, nor had my parents, the seeds of my legacy and its battle were laid in plain straight rows to align with my destiny, a destiny that lay some eighty years into the future.

Now both girls, while they looked nothing at all alike, were beautiful. But Cecelia was of such an inherently sweet disposition that she was the first to be offered a marriage proposal. Perhaps it would not have mattered so much to Amelia had this man Sam Weathers not been a beauty himself. A beauty that Amelia wanted to possess so badly that she resorted to potions and black magic to get it.

Needless to say John was not at all happy with Amelia. He took her aside shortly before the wedding and told her quite sternly that spells and potions were for rank amateurs, and that she had not just a gift but real powers and abilities that would only become lost in senseless words and props. He told her to forget about Sam that he would find her someone just as gifted as she and that they would then produce children of enormous potential.

Amelia was not pacified. She harbored such deep resentments against her father that she could have cared less for his opinions and her feelings of his betrayals toward her were so deep seeded that his promises were only empty echoes. She retreated to her cave, a real place she had found when she was six years old, and began to plot her revenge.

If she, Amelia Dawn Sedler, could not have Sam Wilson Weathers then no one would ever have Sam Weathers. This she declared and set quite literally this vow in a flat sand stone rock. She had discovered quite early on that what one vows and carves in stone is achieved much easier, than when vowed in words and thoughts alone.

It all began innocently enough without any thought being given to Amelia at all at the onset. The general store caught fire. The same store that Sam's family owned and lived above. However, fortune smiled that evening and found no one home and while the Weathers Family was away, a farmer coming back late from the mill spotted the smoke and set off the town's alarm. Although the storeroom and Sam's bedroom were damaged, the store, their home, and the majority of their goods were spared.

The very next day Sam's brother made Sam's usual deliveries for him so that Sam could stay behind and help his father and the volunteers in the community begin the repairs to the store. About a mile out of town the wheel dropped off the horse-drawn buckboard. Fortune in the name of Martha Sedler, smiled on the Weathers Family once more and Jake escaped the accident with nothing more serious than a few minor bruises.

After confirming word of the mishap reached Martha she immediately sought out her first-born daughter Amelia, confronting her in the stables. From what Cecelia and Martha had written in her diaries the meeting went something like this.

Martha told Amelia that she knew she was responsible for the fire and Jake's accident, and she demanded an end to this childish behavior. Amelia cursed her mother calling her powers weak. Martha laughed at her daughter's words and a mule's collar flew off the wall from behind Martha and just inches from Martha's head it stopped and fell to the stable floor.

"I am stronger than you Amelia; you'd best not forget that."

"You're a weak old woman Mama!"

"That's your problem; you always assume and it is your assumptions that will be the end of you young lady."

"No Mama! It's you that assumes that your ways of light are so superior to the true ways."

"Try me Amelia, and you'll be sorry. This I promise you. Now you leave your sister and the Weathers family be!"

Martha turned to leave the stables. A pitchfork from behind and to the side of Amelia, hurled through the air like a javelin heading straight for Martha's back. Martha turned, stopping the pitchfork in mid flight. The pitchfork stayed there hovering in the air its points aimed at Martha's chest. Martha looked from the would-be instrument of her demise, to her daughter then slowly the pitchfork began to turn stopping when its prongs were pointing at her daughter who had the look of a mad woman in her eyes. Suddenly, it began to sail toward Amelia who unable to stop its flight with her mind ducked at the last possible moment. The pitchfork hit the wall with such force that its tips could be seen from the outside.

Amelia stared at her mother with such intensity that Martha wrote in her journal of chills spreading down her spine.

Meeting her daughter's gaze Martha said, "I'll be watching you, little girl." Turning once more she left the stables.

It has been said that Amelia cried that afternoon and her tears unleashed a dam of hatred that immediately turned to a river of icy vengeance.

The day before the wedding both families had been invited to have supper with Sam's maternal grandmother, Patti Graham. Martha was especially tired and apprehensive, and more than anything she wanted to call off this supper. She tried in every way that she could conceive of to convince John to do just that. However, John insisted that the family would attend, and that he would speak to Amelia and warn her to behave, and he did.

It was about the time they were to leave that Amelia disappeared. After a brief search by John and his son Haas and much cursing John loaded his family into the horse drawn carriage and took them on.

After depositing the female members of his family, John went in and made his apologies. He then took his son and went in search of the missing Amelia.

Often times, I picture destiny and the gift as people. I try to imagine the look on their faces when simple human emotions step in the way of their planned greatness. I often try to imagine what these two entities whispered to one another as they saw Amelia lying on her belly in the hedge row not more than a hundred feet from that old wood frame house.

She was polite enough to allow both families to gather there in the front room. She was fearful of her father enough that she allowed him to leave. The polite chatter from that front room drifted out the open windows and filled the summer breeze, while their laughter must have surely torn at Amelia like so many daggers. By all accounts, the families had been together almost a full hour before it began. I often wonder just what thoughts had gone through Amelia's surely tortured mind during this time.

I know that during this time, Martha became more and more anxious as the minutes ticked on by. Her anxiety became so great that she excused herself for a minute and took young Bessie Marie with her out onto the back porch for a breath of fresh air.

Martha and Bessie Marie could not have been out back for more than two or three minutes when Martha heard something inside the house break followed immediately by the boards beneath her feet beginning to shake.

John and his son had started back to the house and could not have been more than ten minutes away when they both heard Martha's voice call John's name and Cecilia's screams. Cracking the whip, John put the horses into full gallop.

Martha grabbed up Bessie Marie and ran off the porch. Realizing that the ground itself was not shaking, she ran with the child to the outhouse. She opened the door and placed her youngest inside instructing the terrified five-year-old to stay put and be quiet. Thank heavens this was a time when children did as they were told without questions or explanation. If they had not, you would not be hearing this story at all.

She approached the house cautiously from the opposite side that Amelia was stationed on forcing her mind to clear in an attempt to locate Amelia. She was very much aware of the screams and sounds of crashing objects coming from inside the house, but it was the cracking sounds of boards and the low rumble that seemed to emanate from under the house that caused her greatest concerns.

Martha followed her third eye and rounding the house, she saw the girl as she was crawling from the hedgerow. Martha pushed her mind into Amelia's with such force that the girl stumbled as she was getting to her feet. Wheeling around she faced her mother.

The rumblings from the house stopped for about thirty seconds. When Martha caught sight of her daughter's face and read the fragments of her demented thoughts, she gasped in horror. Giving Amelia the advantage, thus the rumblings and screams began to rise up once more.

Slowly Amelia walked toward her mother. Unaware that during the brief span the rumblings had ceased, Cecilia had made her way to the window that looked out onto them.

Wisps of smoke started to curl up from the foundation and the roof of the house. Cecilia unaware of the smoke watched as small pebbles started to fly through the air at Martha; some fell just short of their target, most did not.

Martha had never felt the kind of terror she felt when she looked at her daughter. The girl's face was a twisted grotesque mask of rage and demented evil. Try as she might, she could not clear her mind and defend herself, much less the others.

John and Haas saw the smoke as they approached. Drawing up the horses, John jumped down and followed his wife's mental screams.

Frantically, holding onto the window sill, Cecilia searched the yard; her eyes fell on the woodpile. Forcing all thoughts from her mind she looked at the axe, fighting tears from her eyes she screamed for God's forgiveness, as suddenly the axe lifted itself from the woodpile and hurdled end over end as it flew toward her sister's back.

John rounded the house yelling "no" just in time to see the axe impel itself into the back of the one daughter he loved above the others. He heard the growl of the damned, and watched as both Amelia and Martha fell to the ground. He was aware of Cecilia calling Daddy as the wood frame house buckled and fell in on itself amid flames.

Quickly he turned to the burning rubble and began pulling people out. Young Haas had seen more than he'd ever choose to remember and taking a moment to temporarily block the events from his mind, he ran to help his father.

After pulling as many people out as he dared, due to the intense heat of the fire, John went to Amelia and pulled the Axe from her back and handed it to his son instructing him to throw it into the fire. Checking to ensure that his daughter was dead, he lifted her limp body and carried her to the fire that she had set. As great tormented screams tore from his chest and out his throat, he tossed his first-born into the flames.

Martha and Cecilia did not die that day, at least not in body. Martha had been bruised from head to toe; her emotions though had pretty much died within her soul. The truth about her profound gift had been laid bare before her husband and nothing was ever said. Despite the fact that John and Martha grew quietly closer after the events of that day, it is believed that Martha lived on for the next five years solely for the sake of her baby Bessie Marie.

Cecilia had suffered much. Severe burns covered her legs but she never felt the pain, for her back had been broken and she was paralyzed from the waist down. Though she and her mother went on to heal a great many animals and humans, they were never successful in healing her. Even though still a great beauty, Cecilia became a recluse of sorts refusing the courting calls of more than a few young men. She told Bessie Marie once that true love came along only once, and all else would just be a way to fill up empty time and when it came to empty time she had none.

Sam died that day along with his father and grandmother. His mother and brother Jake lived on with no memory of what happened that day. For that the Sedlers were grateful.

The community buried their questions with their dead and soon the tragedy was all but forgotten.

But me, eighty years later I have nightmares about that day, a day I did not live through. For one cannot bury their heritage, their very legacy anymore than they can escape their destiny.................

Prologue (1)

And so it is that I must continue forward and tell you what became of Haas. For, I am sure that the things that directed his life where in part due to his confusion of the events that ended all the possibilities that had once belonged to his sisters. As I told you Haas saw and Haas blocked out that which he had seen. Perhaps it was because he too held all the same abilities he saw reduce life to ashes and splinter his family.

I think it also would have helped if his mother and father had spoke about Amelia to him and had discussed all that he had witnessed and had admitted aloud the abilities that Martha and Cecelia possessed. But talking is not something that those of that time did often or well. Lies and secrets within a family, when laid bare for all to see, were never discussed. And perhaps these secrets, these lies by omission, were not discussed because to do so would have been to admit things for which John and Martha held no words.

As I said before, back then in those days, in that place, little was known about the gift. Little was known about emotions, and all was framed around the basic belief that men were the heads of the family, the undisputed leaders, the strongest, the smartest, so perhaps the success of the secret having laid in silence so many years, was a threat to John's place within the family, his place at its head.

I also feel that had Haas been talked to in honesty about his sister Amelia, had the errors of her ways and her gifts been openly discussed and communicated to him in words and deeds and set out as example of truths, then the house, the events that built it and filled it and forced me forward into a role I really would have rather avoided and framed a legacy that is less than rosy, would have never come to pass. Perhaps, then a house would have been a house, and happiness would have reigned there and maybe just maybe children of love would have been born and all of us in this family would have been stronger and wiser.

Then again, it takes what it takes to make us who we are. And the perceptions that we have are born of the realities that we face. It would have been lovely to have a strong love story with a happy ending emerge from the tale of Haas and his beloved Matilda.

WALTZING MATILDA

There was once a place that was perpetually decades behind the times; up until the computer age, which came to this area about ten years after it came to the rest of the state.

Before, this county, nestled deep in the heart of Tennessee, played host to one city and three small towns, back before it could boast of a population well over sixty thousand. Way back even before it could boast of industry, back about the time the university was starting to become a little more than a dream, this was just a place known, if at all, as Spirit Springs in Cedars County, Tennessee.

Cedars County was once a place that held the bragging rights to the finest farm lands in all the state. It was also known far and wide for its fine craftsmen. Cedars county was a place that was comprised of four sleepy little towns and communities far too numerous to mention. These communities served as micro towns, if you will. Believe it or not, there were people born in communities with funny little names like Cat's-eye Junction, Nowhere, Muddy Branch, Lazy Mules Falls, Whispering Springs, Bored Valley (I kid you not the spelling is right on this one), and Spirit Springs to name a few, who lived their entire lives without ever having left their community. And why should they when these communities had an all-purpose general store that was also a post office and a one room school house that in many cases doubled as a church on Sunday mornings. They also had the grist mills, sorghum mills, lumber yards, blacksmiths and, of course, the cemeteries.

In these tired little communities, men worked back-breaking labor from sunup to sundown six days a week taking the Sabbath off to attend church, visit with the neighbors, whittle, and rest up for the week ahead. While the women worked from an hour before sunup and at least two hours after sundown tackling everything from the menial, including making the clothing and the quilts, to the back-breaking alongside the men all while raising the children and the chickens six days a week and taking on cooking, cleaning and darning on their day of rest or the Sabbath.

I told you that this was a place suspended somehow in a web of time, a place where up until the 1950s, the calendars of fashion and music, as well as changing social mores, ran at least ten years behind the rest of the world. Yet, somehow the fifties, with its televisions, poodle skirts, bobby socks and rock 'n' roll, arrived on time and with the exception of car styles changing, the fifties and all they embodied stayed around until the 1970s. But I'm getting ahead of myself, aren't I?

It was the roaring twenties up north and the roar's echo was just beginning to be heard in the big cities in the south. But in small towns and the even smaller sleepy communities of the south, that roar was but a whisper.

Women in the big cities were finding their voices and tasting their freedom, some were daring to take on jobs outside the home and dreaming of careers. They were indulging generations of pent up thirsts for education and putting off marriage until their twenties. They were standing bold in their dress and relationships, seeking input and daring to stand against all that had been accepted quietly as a woman's lot in life by their mothers and grandmothers before them.

Women in this time and those places were raising hemlines and hairlines while indulging in cosmetics and excessive jewelry.

However, in Cedars County, Tennessee, time stood on as still as the cedars and oaks that crowded the mountains. The ladies there were unquestionably southern in their quiet complacent acceptance of all that was around them. Any thirst, any hunger, any daring that may have stirred in their souls never once came forward. Like their hope, their desires stayed buried deep within their souls, where generations of oppression, breeding and grooming had covered it.

While in the big cities throughout the United States where fashion became more daring, the women of Cedars County still wore gingham and flour sack dresses a proper two inches above the ankle. They wore these dresses in the hot summer fields, over the Thursday washboards, and in the humid kitchens. On Sundays, these dresses were made proper with an attachable lace collar and a single strand of pearls or a gold locket. A daub of petroleum jelly to the lips was their only attempt at cosmetics. They grew their hair long and brushed it each night until it gleamed, and each morning found them once again winding it tightly about their heads.

In their relationships the women were quiet, speaking to their husbands only when it was absolutely necessary, accepting their man's word as law. Any idea, thoughts, wants, or opinions were kept deeply locked away inside themselves, sometimes where education and few pennies were found-- all that they kept locked away revealed itself in diaries.

It was in this time and this place and in these ways that pretty Matilda Mae Henry was born and raised. She was a wanted and welcomed blessing in her home, coddled by her father who struggled on alone to raise her when her mother died quietly and mysteriously while Matilda was just about two years into the beginning of her life.

Also in this time and this place, a young man called Haas Sedler, about the age of twelve was being raised with a promise and being taught his gift while he and his father worked off and on constructing a very special home for young Haas and his future bride.

Education for females in those days and in these communities rarely went beyond the fourth grade, and unless he was from a well off family, the boy rarely went beyond the sixth grade. But with Matilda, her father pushed her all the way through the eighth grade, all the while filling her head with Bible verses and Bible promises.

Though her father had been a heavy drinker before Matilda's birth, he abstained afterwards with a zealousness that bordered on fanaticism. In short, the man who lacked much in the way of money and education did all his mind could conceive of to protect his daughter from a fool's drunken promise, even though, in the back of his mind he'd known since shortly before her birth that Matilda's destiny had been carved in stone. Yet he held hope for escape, after all the Good Book promised that hope was the essence of things not seen, and to his way of thinking, nothing was as unseen as an avenue of escape.

While the big cities had their speak easies and social clubs, Spirit Springs had its church socials and Saturday night barn dances. And that is where Haas found her, his promised Matilda.

He spied her standing in the corner of the barn while fiddles whined and couples danced, while the smells of early summer whiffed in the air. Hass noticed that she seemed somehow lost standing there in her pretty gingham dress, her auburn hair arranged just so that it framed her strong and beautiful face with its defiant chin and full pouty lips. He noted that she stood straight adding volumes to her slender tallness. Haas saw her as if through a haze; she seemed invisible to all others around her and lost in a trance oblivious to all that was taking place around her.

What he didn't know was that she felt his stare. She felt him in her head, trying to move through her thoughts. And as he tried to shuffle through her mind, pictures tried to flash before her mind's eye, she held them back. But Haas, a man so aware of all that he was and all that he knew, was so taken in by her beauty that he barely sensed her reluctance. He barely noted her ability to block him from her. Feeling his soul, his heart move in such raw purity, Matilda looked up and across the room where she met his great, intensely beautiful brown eyes with her own sapphire blue ones.

Never before had anyone feigned a resistance to Haas, and he knew right then and there that she was the one his father had told him would fulfill a promise. Not taking his eyes from hers, he made his way across the crowded dance floor not noticing that people parted a wave before him.

He was twenty-eight, she was just sixteen when he took her hand and amid dueling fiddles, they waltzed the night away.

So as destiny had ordained and been satisfied by a fool's drunken vow, Haas took Matilda for his very own in the early fall of 1923 and placed her in a home, a three story antebellum, he'd built for her before he knew her. She waltzed with him over the hardwood floors as Indian summer breezes billowed through the lace curtains. And for a while, just as promised, they were happy, and destiny fulfilled. Yet, destiny is seldom so one-dimensional.

It has been said since the beginning of time by those in supposed authority that unless one is prepared; (as if one could ever be) the full impact of the gift can drive a sane man crazy. It has also been said since before the beginning, (hence the war in heaven) that the gift in the wrong hands could spell an end to the world as we know it.

Since I have witnessed the gift and its aftermath personally, I believe both sayings to be seeded in truth.

Needless to say, Haas was no ordinary man. Physically speaking he stood out as he was just over six foot six inches and his weight was a full rock solid two fifty or better. He had been well educated both scholastically and in what we would now call the PSI arts. He had raven black hair that shown almost blue in the sun, and his eyes were so brown that in moments of intensity they almost glowed amber. Women had quietly noticed his beauty for he was a creature of pure beauty. Since his childhood, the women had stayed away from him as if overwhelmed by his strength, while in fact they were ever fearful of his eyes. For he had eyes that seemed to burn the very souls of all those he gazed at.

In becoming the wife of Haas Sedler, Matilda had gone where no other woman would have dared. It was because of her marriage to Haas, that all of her friends dropped away from her. But in those early days of pure love and love's pure bliss, I doubt she noticed or cared.

Haas had no friends--never had and never would. However, men respected him; I suspect more out of fear than anything else. You see Haas had never been a violent man at least until his marriage, even though not one person could ever recall having seen him find anger, before or during the marriage. Truth is the only real memory of his temperament was how quiet he was. It has been said of Haas that when one shook his hand, one could feel their thoughts being tossed around inside their heads like so many socks in a drawer. These were the types of things that the God-fearing men of Spirit Springs did not understand, and if for no other reason, they held a healthy respect for Haas, while unconsciously shunning him.

In order to understand why men kept a healthy distance from Haas, you must understand that southern people then, and even now, have a healthy respect for things they cannot understand, things that cannot be explained, and just how Haas had moved those boulders at the age of sixteen, or at any other age for that matter without touching them, no one could explain. All the same to their credit rather than fear him, the men folk held a healthy respect for him. Perhaps they accepted him because with all his differences and all that the family had possessed, which had set them apart, the family had paid a heavy price. I doubt that feelings in the community would have been as respectful or gracious had the Sedler family flourished without the shockingly tragic events that had unfolded in the family.

What I suspect no one could have known or understood was that Haas truly feared those men. Oh, yes, it is true that whoever possesses the gift, fears a great many things. Maybe that's because there are no proper schools for the gift's development, no manual one can trust-- just a lot of beliefs and superstitions, many of which unfounded. Haas feared these men and their religions, he feared their God, he feared their understanding of Satan, and he envied them their precious belief in heaven.

Haas' father had taught him a great deal about his gift, but Haas had always felt that there was something not right, something almost bad that his father had been keeping from him. As is true of all of us who bear the weight of the gift, even when we are fortunate enough to have experienced teachers from birth, Haas had developed his gift through instinct. With great and conflicting dismay, he had watched as the older of his elder twin sisters followed her gift to insanity and beyond, while the younger had learned to live with the heavy price the gift had extracted from her.

Then there was his younger sister...

Well, Haas found that his baby sister Bessie Marie, whom he'd learned to accept and love, was a lot more gifted than she would ever admit, truth be told he saw a lot of Bessie Marie in Matilda. He would never be sure, until the bitter end, but at times he suspected Matilda was quietly gifted. But these times of suspicion were just brief moments, quiet glimpses as it were. Glimpses, which his intense feelings of love for her never allowed him to fully view.

It occurred to Haas before the first year of their marriage was complete that the only thing he knew for sure about Matilda was that she must surely walk in light. The same light that had kept him from reading his mother's and sisters' thoughts must be what kept him from reading her thoughts as well. At least that's what his father had told him about people whose thoughts he could not easily read, "They walk in light ,Son."

He repeated those words to himself as he remembered reading that women were a lot different from men. Books of his day said that obvious differences aside, a woman was of a completely different stock than a man. A weaker stock more prone to fits of hysteria, and their thinking was different, more irrational. While Haas wasn't sure that all this was true, partly because he remembered that his mother was a very strong and sure person, maybe her strength had come from her dousing of the gift, but at the end of his conflicting thoughts he finally consented that maybe there was some element of truth to all that he had read.

Since his upbringing and education helped notat all to answer with surety the basic questions that for some reason seemed important to him in these early days with his bride, his doubts and insecurity grew. And as these questions and feelings grew and collided with the words his gift fed to him, he withdrew himself inches each day from the woman he loved enough and wanted to be his friend.

Matilda had noticed his withdrawal. In a way she couldn't understand, it was a relief to her. She knew without ever once having been told of his gift, just as she knew without once having been told that she too possessed a version of the same gift. And though she had always been able to read thoughts, she'd never been as bold as he. For no one had ever been able to feel her enter their private world. She had also grown tired of instinctively fighting his mind from hers.

And she was scared, though the totality of her fear escaped her, she knew what scared her most of all was that she could no longer catch glimpses of his soul-- a soul that she loved-- much less read snatches of his thoughts. Purely by instinct, she knew that he must never be able to find the Bible verses hidden in her mind or the Bible promises buried deep within her heart. So it was that in the end as he withdrew so did she.

Shortly after Haas and Matilda had wed, he'd hired one Fanny Rae to clean their home and do up the laundry for he did not want his beautiful Waltzing Matilda to become old and bent before her time, like so many of the other young brides of the community he'd noticed in the past. What he hadn't realized at the time was that his beautiful young bride was destined to age ten years for every two years of marriage.

Fanny Rae was considered white trash by the community; a community that was quick to forget that she had been born a banker's daughter and raised in the proper genteel ways of a southern lady. It had been a moment of young, even childish, passionate and reckless abandonment that had ruined her, so to speak. Things being what they were and the past a kaleidoscope of emotions, happenings, half truths and outright lies, Fanny Rae, with her pure soul and good heart, was destined to live with her mistakes and because of her mistakes she would become old and bent before her time. In the end, all she knew for sure was that she had married bad and had paid a truly heavy price not to have had one moment of joy in her adult life thanks to those rash choices.

Fanny Rae was not in the least bit afraid of Mr. Haas and what she called his personal demons. As for judgment, well a woman like Fanny Rae, who had seen the Demon Rum take her husband behind the barn on Christmas Eve, her oldest son in a barroom brawl in a far off place called Nashville, her second boy at the hands of a whiskey revenuer, and was now waiting for her baby boy to die at the hands of the state because of his drunken passions, she was not one to make or hold judgments against anyone. No, Fanny Rae just couldn't see how a woman like her could rightly pass judgment on any man and his own demons whatever that may be.

What I think Fanny Rae may have lacked the words to say, was that constantly he shuffled through her thoughts. His eyes beheld an unspeakable horror within them. His hair-- that raven black hair slowly began to show strands of intense silver. She also noted after the fact that he had turned colder toward his precious Matilda, becoming verbally hostile with her.   Even though he went into that second root cellar often and stayed hours on end praying against it, he knew that Destiny had authored this slow separation from all that he loved. The gift which had in its own way lay claim to every single member of his family save one, the same gift that demanded the building of this house was now demanding his beautiful Waltzing Matilda, and he loved her too much to give her away without his own fight.

Fanny Rae worked for the couple six days a week and worried about them on the seventh. While she wasn't sure that her prayers would avail them much, never-the-less she prayed each night for God's help. She watched in silence as Miss Matilda went from joyous young bride to a miserably lonely and despondent young woman. She thought in her mind that the changes in Miss Matilda were because Mr. Haas was spending more and more time in the second locked root cellar-- the one she'd been sternly warned against entering on the very first day of work. Of course, she could see that Mr. Haas was changing.

Fanny Rae is quoted in a grand jury report as saying, "It was a slow change but it was a powerful one. I could almost smell the evil a growin' in him. Of coursin' with me, he was still nice and all. But that is what made it all kind a more scary if 'n' you know what I mean."

Of course Fanny Rae had no way of knowing how right she was about the true evil that surrounded not only Haas but Matilda as well. She had no way of knowing about the price extracted from those to whom much has been given.

In that time and in that place, women shared very little with one another. However, in the case of Fanny Rae and Matilda words didn't have to be exchanged in order to be said. For Matilda quietly entered Fanny Rae's mind in order to make her needs known. Because unknowingly, Fanny Rae had the eyes that opened onto the soul of a woman who understood more about demons and destiny than anyone in all of Cedars County, Matilda felt warmed knowing that someone with whom some understanding of what was happening to her was in her life.

And Fanny Rae did know. She knew from Matilda's sweet beginnings to her quiet acceptance and all the way to the bitter resignation of her fate. Fanny Rae Wills had somehow known Matilda's destiny. God help her she'd known. And it is that knowledge that would haunt her to her grave some thirty years later.

Despite the prayers of Fanny Rae, and the best efforts on behalf of both Haas and Matilda, his gift and its unnecessary yet willingly chosen allegiances, grew with each passing season of their marriage forcing him to the root cellar for longer and longer periods of time and forcing Matilda to recall those Bible verses and promises almost to obsession. Although her mind was a blank to him her emotions were not. His gift picked up on her obsession though he knew not what that obsession was. His gift gave to him a third eye that he kept trained on her every movement at all times. While her gift thankfully alerted her to this, it also helped her come to the painful and terrifying realization that she was a prisoner in her own home, and worse still in her own mind. And now there was no longer any chance for her to escape and go to church as she craved even though she knew that it would have done her no good.

For you see, religions now as well as then, born of and in the back water south, could not and do not accept the gift as existing, much less demons in the forms in which they truly do exist, which is in the hearts and minds of everyone found in their actions and words. They don't understand that one stands to serve light or darkness by the actions they take and the attitudes and injustices they choose to hold onto to. In so doing, they fail to see that demons are not beings with horns and pointy tails but rather aberrations of the people that they see in the mirror.

Haas knew that Fanny Rae, though unable to ever put into conscious thought or word, was aware of that his gift had become an entity and bore witness to the way it fed on Matilda. What he did not know was that Matilda was also aware and fighting in her own remote, desperate and futile ways.

None the less, he watched and was aware as during that first year, her sparkling laughter slowly faded away and was gone. It truly hurt him that she no longer smiled; there was not even a trace of one by the end of the second year. When the third year dawned on their union, he realized that he couldn't remember with any clarity the last time they had danced. Yet, he felt powerless to take her in his arms and attempt to bring back the passion of the first year. By the end of the fourth year, she cried often. His third eye made him painfully aware of this fact and it tore at his soul like a fever that he was without power to quench. By the beginning of their fifth year together, a dark and ominous cloud settled over their perfect home and Destiny's perfect mistress.

What happens at night in the home of two married people is still a closely guarded secret in the rural south. In the roaring twenties in Cedars County, no one thought about it, no one allowed themselves to care. All anyone knew was that after five years of marriage, Haas and Matilda had no children and that fact did give rise to polite whispers.

It was long about the sixth year, a scant few months before a falling Wall Street would make headlines around the world, even in Spirit Springs, when Fanny Rae came to work to find that Miss Matilda's pretty auburn hair had turned completely white at some point between her leaving on Saturday afternoon and her coming in that Monday morning. Not only was her hair white, but Miss Matilda either couldn't or wouldn't speak. Not a word for two long months.

Up until her death some thirty years late,r Fanny Rae often spoke of the day the silence was broken. She reported to work to find Miss Matilda sitting in the parlor rocker. She could recall how the warm spring breezes billowed through the pink lace curtains, and how Miss Matilda still wore her robe and her long white hair hung loose and free in tangled disarray. Matilda's once beautiful face was bruised and a daub of dried blood hung to her swollen lower lip.

Fanny Rae said she rushed out to the kitchen for a cool pan of water and a soft rag and came back into the parlor and began cleaning Miss Matilda up. Then suddenly Matilda caught her eyes with her own and in a voice that sent shivers down Fanny Rae's spine Matilda said, "It took me. Now I'm with child. What will I do? Whatever will I do?"

In the backwoods, south of today spousal abuse is often still all too sadly accepted as normal, and unfortunately in some regions it's even expected, though thankfully that view is slowly changing. However in the 1920's, in Spirit Springs no one dared care, caring was the one thing that got people killed. A house was a man's castle, his wife and children mere property. And unless someone was killed no one wanted to know, much less pass open judgment.

Fanny Rae said nothing, experience had taught her that other than to gossip no one cared or would have listened. Besides, she knew from some place down deep within her very soul that Mr. Haas could not have done this awful and terrible thing. She knew that he cherished his Waltzing Matilda far too much.

From that day forward when she came into work, she would always find Mr. Haas sitting on the front porch staring deep into space. He never spoke to Fanny Rae again and as far as she knew he never again went into his cellar. Never again did Fanny Rae find Miss Matilda with her hair up or see her dressed in anything but her nightclothes. Without words, she forced bits of nourishment on both the Mr. and the Mrs... instinctively she knew that they were grateful. Yet, outside their home while both of them lived on, she said nothing.

It bothered Fanny Rae that there was no one she could go to that would or could help them. Each night, she went down the list of people she knew or even knew of, hoping against all hope that a new name would come to her. But it was no use. Haas' sister had gotten herself married and had moved to someplace called Knoxville for a spell and Fanny Rae hadn't a clue as to how to go about finding her, though she did watch the mail real close. And then there was Matilda's father but he'd up and moved off to parts unknown about five years back. All the other folks in town were scared of Mr. Haas, so that meant to her way of thinking that taking care of them was up to her.

One Saturday late, she picked up her pay envelope from the kitchen table where it always mysteriously appeared just before she took her leave and bade her employers a farewell. What she never saw was the one thing she feared the most.

Haas watched as Fanny Rae walked down the drive and up the road; he thought to himself that she was a really good person. A bit misguided perhaps, but none the less a good person.

As she disappeared from view, the expression on his face changed to one of almost horror. In his mind, he pleaded as he heard the cellar door around back open. He could not see it not even with his third eye when the chill of it walked passed him. But he pleaded with it none the less.

He felt the remaining black hair on his head turn silver as he watched the front door beside him open as if on its own. He heard what he thought to be the gift utter, "Betray me in my unholy home with Christ! I think not!" As the front door slammed shut breaking the glass.

Haas was aware of Destiny reaching up and slapping him in the face as it cried out, "You Fool! You Fool!"

He tried to get to his feet but he could not.

He heard her screams. He cried. He heard things break. He tried to find his voice but found instead a pathetic croak.

He heard growling, he heard hissing, and he could almost feel his bones break as he heard Matilda's cries.

Even though he could not move, he was forced with his third eye to watch as his sweet Matilda was thrown about her parlor like a limp rag doll.

His heart broke, his eyes cried, and his mind prayed to the very Christ his mother had spoke about and his father had warned him against.

The gift demands so very much, while when directed in the wrong ways, it ultimately gives so very little. The gift, used right or wrong, has the power to alter destiny.

The gift can become almost human in its emotions. In its anger, it is capable of destroying the very things it seeks to find. At least the gift does when in the wrong hands.

After church on Sunday, Fanny Rae stopped by the house to check up on Haas and Matilda and force upon them nourishment as had become her custom in recent weeks. When she returned that Sunday afternoon ,she found Haas sitting where she had left him the evening before looking closer to a hundred than thirty some odd years.

Before she walked up onto the porch she knew. But with weak legs she walked on up and into the house anyway.

Haas was aware of her screams; he wished he could scream too. He forgave her and envied her ability to run passed him and off the front porch.

The house still stands in all its infamous glory. Although Haas' sister, my grandmother, was appointed the guardian of his sizeable estate, not one bit of work, other than the replacement of the broken glass, and the addition of electricity has been done to the old house. Yet neither time nor weather has taken a toll. The old white house with its green tin roof still stands tall, proud and most beautifully alluring.

Haas' root cellar was found locked on that day back in 1929 and not once in all these years has anyone bothered to open it. I think that even those not blessed with this gift knew exactly what horrors lay resting behind that rusting lock.

My grandmother, Bessie Marie did rent the house a handful of times over the years. No one ever stayed more than six months except for that self-proclaimed new age psychic a few years back. I think she lasted a full year. But in the end, she too left like all the others, in the dead of the night asking us to send her possessions on to her.

They all left, some after just a couple of days. Their stories are all the same, whether they stayed days or months, they heard distant far off screams in the middle of the night, they suffered horrid nightmares, the walls seemed to breathe, and the ceilings appeared to sweat. Then of course there are the sounds of breaking glass, windows that open and close at will, and yes, oh yes, there's that ever-present bone freezing chill.

It's 1994 now, and Haas has never been formally charged in the death of his wife and won't be until he recovers. He's been locked away all these years in the state mental hospital, bound in his own prison of silence; doomed to relive the gift's vengeance over and over for his crime against the dark allegiances of the gift.

The first, last and only time I've been in that house was all it took. Matilda's chill is still in my bones. Yet, I know that soon I must confront the demons that my uncle Haas unleashed there. And to be honest as I work and as I grow, I pray that what I know to be my destiny will never be necessary.

When I look from my grandmother's windows at the house or sit in her front yard and stare across the road at it, I can hear it calling to me. Yet, I fear more from my nightmares than anything else that a part of the gift that I have waits there to drive me mad.

How do I know what has become of Uncle Haas? How do I know what torments his mind and how do I know the answers to all the questions that tells me he's innocent of all the charges that await him?

I know because I've been a welcomed guest in his mind more times than I care to think. And even now, even with all the knowledge of the gift I have I am powerless until called, to help him undo the dark side's hold.

I hear his warnings daily. And what scares me the most about where he took his gift is the punishment for his crime against it.

What was his crime you ask?

Haas' only crime against the gift was bringing his Waltzing Matilda the Bible her mind cried out to him for. The way I see it his only crime was a final act of love.

Prologue (2)

Although, in my humble opinion, the story of Haas and his Waltzing Matilda in the end was a story of true love, it is also a story of caution. No matter who you are, you have to be careful of whom you spiritually serve. Family, bloodlines, genetics and all the rest be damned. It is whom you serve that renders the endings you walk away with at the end of the day.

It is also a story that tells us that to truly love, we must first be willing to sacrifice all that we know--especially when we know the consequences. And I do believe that Haas knew the consequences that would befall him if he went out to the old barn and rifled through the trunks that were there and brought in the Bible that his mother had given to Amelia when she was a child.

Shortly after Haas was sent away to begin his life-long sentence of catatonia in a state hospital(not because he could not have afforded a private one but because he was believed to be a criminal so he was condemned to the state hospital), my grandmother Bessie Marie and her beloved husband, Oscar Hammonds, returned to the family farm-- all 900 acres of it. On the land opposite Haas' part at an angle across from his house, my grandfather rebuilt the Sedler family home for his wife adding several beautiful high A-frame arcs.

And so, it was within the shadow of my legacy that my mother and eventually myself, were raised to rise up to meet our own destinies, to wage battles or to succumb to false promises or what I hope for me, has been a time and a place of rising above false promises and setting a new height for my destiny.

CIRCLE CLOSES

I was born old. At least that's what my Granny and Pa used to always say. I was born old to a Mama who died having me and a Daddy who blamed me. He signed me over to the state; the state signed me over to my Granny and Pa who needed me. Mama had been their only child; you'd have thought that they would have blamed me instead of welcoming me.

I was brought from the hospital in the winter of 1963 to their home in a community called Spirit Springs, in the county of Cedars, in the state of Tennessee. There I grew wrapped in their love and tender devotion amid 900 of the best acres of farmland in middle Tennessee. I was surrounded by cows, pigs, chickens, and ducks. I spent my days playing in the warm breezes of three out of four seasons all the while staring across the road at the three-story white house with the green tin roof.

I can't remember a time when I did not read, and I don't recall a single day when I did not put words onto paper.

I guess I was about four when I realized that the three of us in this happy little home spoke without saying a word; we could carry on entire conversations without having to be in the same room. I guess that's why I don't recall ever being lonely or feeling lost like so many people I hear talking about today.

Yes, the three of us were close, and I was happy. I asked Granny once when I was real small why she didn't blame me for Mama's death the way my Daddy did. I'll never forget the way she turned off the stove and walked over to the kitchen table where I was sitting, and took my little hands into her soft work worn ones. Looking me straight in the eye she said, "Child, the Lord never takes what he don't give back ten thousand times over. And you child, are mine and Pa's saving grace. That's why we named you Grace."

It was that incident that day that pretty much sums up the way that I was raised. Everything came to a halt when I had a problem or a question. I came first. Oh I did plenty wrong and was the first to be told when I did. But I also did plenty right and was the first to be praised when I did.

Yes, I knew love, true love, my whole life.

I knew my calling too. I can't remember a single day when my Pa didn't work with me on my levitations, that's what he called moving objects with my mind. And I knew just as much about roots and herbs and their healing properties as my Granny by the time I started school. Both my Granny and Pa worked with me on reading thoughts and finding objects.

I was Grace Hope, their saving grace and their one last hope for the gift to come full circle and become truly good again. To that end, Granny and Pa saw me to church every Sunday and read the Bible to me every night.

Granny told me about her brother Haas and his wife Matilda, taking great pains to explain just why I should avoid that big white house across the road until just the right time. She also told me of her sisters Amelia and Cecilia, and I could tell how it pained her to tell me of the insanity that came from her side of the family that was my heritage.

Pa told me all about his growing up years in Knox County, Tennessee. He shared with me all the stories about his family and their experiences with the gift. Good, quiet, peaceful, God-filled experiences.

What I think was hardest for Granny and Pa to tell me about was my Mama. Mama had the gift, she had it strong, and she let it lead her. The gift should be guided, but Mama was so head strong that she let it lead her into a world of hurtful pain. Just like her aunt and uncle before her.

I still don't know the whole story though I know it had something to do with that house. I could always use the gift to find out all those loose ends, but I probably never will. You see it pained my Granny and Pa just to tell me what the few details they wanted me to know, so I saw no reason, even now—even after all I have been through in these recent months, in part because of Mama to push things out into the open. It is best sometimes to let evil lie in order to honor goodness.

There are many things that I believe in. I believe in holiness and in purity. I believe in hope and grace and in heaven and in a hell of our own making. I believe that salvation is something we earn with each day that we live and the choices that we make, and I also believe that salvation is found in each thought, deed and action. I have come to believe that all too often, for the common man, his hell is right here on earth. I have come to know all the things that my Uncle Haas envied, and I have been touched by all that he feared. I have known evil and have been touched by the physical form of evil personified.

I studied the gift under all its proper names. I have met gifted ones and charlatans alike. I have tried to persuade those who dabble to not open their minds to the very things that are so dangerous. I have argued with preachers and other holy men who would deny the gift, excuse it, ignore or condemn it for they know not what evil they allow by their oversights, or for that matter what goodness straight from the Bible they cast aside.

As you may know my story really began a hundred years ago when Granny's father opened his mind and heart allowing darkness to descend upon him and his heirs. It all came full circle about six months ago when I Grace Hope stood alone with the gift I held to fulfill a purpose, rather than another's promise, before I could ever seek to fulfill all my own hopes and dreams.

Such simple dreams of a loving husband and a family of my own would be denied until I fulfilled that purpose--until I stood alone veiled in fear and insecurity to face my destiny while breaking a pact and undoing my heritage.

Pa died ten years back, and I've missed him terribly. But Granny went on teaching me. She acted as my sounding board when I needed to lay out all the conflicting and often times confusing things I had read about the gift. Often she'd explain just why science was wrong and she was quick to put down certain theories that were accepted as fact by calling them myths.

Toward the end of her life she told me that true knowledge of the gift came from day-to-day experience. Not just my own experiences but the experiences of all those who had lived before.

We were sitting out in the yard one day when I asked her if she believed that all people had at least a hint of the gift. The smile she gave me then and there was one full of pride as she pointed to the house across the road she answered my question, "Just why do you think no one has ever been able to stay in that house?"

Sadly in January of 1995, Granny passed from this plane of existence on to the next. I was at a conference in Nashville some ninety miles away that night. I had just fallen asleep alone in my motel room when I was awakened by my Granny's smell. It permeated the room.

I knew then. I was getting ready to leap up out of bed and throw on my clothes when I saw the light. Not much more than a pen light at first, at the foot of my bed, and as I watched, it grew bigger. And then bathed in the whitest of lights they both materialized. My Granny and Pa stood there at the foot of that bed.

Pa smiled as Granny spoke, "we're together again Grace. The time has come for you to use all that we have instilled in you."

"Gracie, your grandmother and I will be with you as you go forth and purify your heritage."

"Erase the evil Grace so that we can all be together again. We'll be not far from you until you're done."

Then just as suddenly as they had appeared they were gone, and for the first time in my life, I knew just what it was to be mortally alone.

Needless to say I was home in less than three hours to confirm what I already knew with such clarity to be true. There are often times when I wish that I weren't right, and this had been one of those times.

I had no more than hung up the phone from calling authorities than it rang, and I was told that my Uncle Haas had just passed on. He was once and for all after sixty-five years freed from his self made prison of silence and nightmares. It may sound strange, even cruel to some of you but I was happy for him--happy to see his nightmare come to an end.

On January 15, 1995, I wrote these words in my journal: Now at long last John and Martha Sedler have all their children together again. Pa has his beloved at his side, and for the first time in my thirty-two years of life, I must awake to go forward alone..... Now I can say that I know the pain of loneliness. I wish I couldn't.

As the winter dragged on, I spent most of my time alone in the living room where I had grown up staring across the road at Haas and Matilda's house. I had inherited it all, both the estates of Granny and Pa as well as Haas. The lawyer was quick to point out that I was set for life. He had called me one fortunate young lady. He pointed out that I was free to sell Haas' house and that I should consider doing just that now that it was a buyer's market. At that time, I had wished that I was truly free to do just that.

For the next four months I read the Bible promises and books about the gift and hauntings. I also watched the big white house with the green tin roof as the snow fell on it and then melted slowly off. I noticed how at night it seemed to glow; its numerous windows were like giant black eyes watching me. I honestly believe that's what it did. It watched me. It beckoned me. It mocked me. And I know that it laughed at me for there were some nights when I was awakened from a deep sound sleep by menacing laughter.

My solitude was only briefly interrupted by a few very close and personal friends. One of them was a Catholic priest who was intrigued by the gift and all topics related to it.

We had traded banter and books in the past, and the few times I saw him during this period we talked more seriously. From the beginning of that dark year ,I had seriously debated with myself the merits of having him with me when I fulfilled my destiny. I'll never forget our conversation the night I asked him about the possibility of joining me.

We were sitting in Granny's living room; the house across the road staring out over the night at us, watching us. I imagine it was listening, perhaps even mocking us. He was sipping his coffee when I finally found the nerve to ask him.

"Father, do you believe in possession?"

"The Church teaches the possibilities of it."

"That's not what I asked Father. Do you personally believe that people, objects, houses; even land can be possessed?"

"It's possible Grace."

"Anything is possible Father. I asked you whether or not you believe it does in fact happen."

"I have never witnessed a possession. Though I have been taught to believe it happens. I have also even been taught prayers for just such an event. I do believe in evil, so yes, I guess if I got serious about it, I would have to say that I do believe in the power of possession."

"Does that idea scare you at all?"

"How do you mean Grace?"

"If I told you that evil was in every board and every nail of a house and that I was going there to face that evil down, would you be reluctant to go with me?"

"I would of course hope that you were wrong. But if you felt in your heart that you needed me, I would go."

"How strong is your faith Father?"

"How strong is yours Grace?"

"There is not one doubt in my mind that light can over take darkness, Father. There is also not one doubt in my mind that from time to time it is possible for darkness to overtake light."

"I believe in God the Father, and in Christ his son. I believe in the Blessed Virgin and in the powers of saints and angels without number. Most importantly, I believe that there is nothing in or out of this world that these powers cannot beat into submission if called upon to do so. Faith can move mountains Grace."

"And now we are back where we began Father."

"Do you feel that you need me Grace?"

"Yes Father I do."

"Then I'll be there."

"Do I need to convert first?"

"No I'll save your immortal soul later."

We laughed.

There was one other incident just prior to the day the Father and I had set aside for my fulfillment. That's what I had taken to calling it. Fulfillment Day. Sounds almost insane now.

It was long about the end of March--warm for the season--when this old beat up station wagon pulled into my driveway. I watched from the side door as a rather lonely looking girl about my age stepped from the car. I sensed the depression that hung about her like a cloak. I couldn't read her thoughts which told me that whether or not she knew it, we had a lot in common. However, I was able to discern her spirit and it was not one of peace.

I stepped out onto the carport and looked at a very pretty woman as she approached me rather hesitantly. The only vibration I got from her was a strong one of marriage.

"Hi. Can I help you?"

"Just promise me you won't think that I am crazy."

"I promise. My name is Grace."

"I'm...a... I'm Sam."

"It's a warm day today isn't it?"

"I..I was beginning to think that winter would never leave."

"Would you like to come in?"

"No...I had a dream...Sometimes they come true... If I can remember the details...But, the one I had last night it was so clear... I had to drive by to be sure..."

"You dreamed about the house across the road didn't you?"

"Yes."

"And it was bad wasn't it?"

"It was evil Grace... Don't go... Please don't go."

"Do you know anything about me?"

"No...I only know that sometimes when you're too close to something you don't always see the signs until it's too late...So please don't go."

I reached out to touch her. I had to. I saw so much pain and fear written in her eyes and across her face that I couldn't see anything else except...

"You can't do it Sam."

"Can't do what?"

"You can't kill yourself."

She jumped back from me like she had been shot. Perhaps she had. Sometimes I get glimpses that scare me in their urgency and I speak in words and tones that show that urgency and scare even me in their harshness. But I will never forget the look in her eyes. It was look of pure betrayal. Kind of like a deer that thinks it's safe there in the darkness then the lights hit it.

"I knew that I was crazy to come here."

"No, Sam you weren't." She turned and started to walk away. "Sam, please don't go. I want to help you."

With those last words from my mouth she ran back to her car. I ran after her. I had to touch that car. I did just before she pulled out. I yelled, "I'll pray for you!"

Her eyes. I have seen so much that I wish I had never been able to see. The eyes are truly the windows to the soul, and never before in one soul had I ever seen that much pain and loneliness. And it was because of those very things that I saw that I knew that she had been set apart from all the rest of us. There are a few souls who walk amongst us, strong souls who endure much as easily as the rest of endure little, and these specially selected souls endure while waiting to be tapped. They are set aside so that no real harm can come to them until their moment of destiny, I should clarify and say no real harm other than by their own hand. And it was this knowledge that filled me with the pain and isolation that she felt that she knew as her existence. I wish I could have told her in that instance that this isolation was to keep her pure for the job that lay ahead. A job, a purpose that she had agreed to before she came to this earth.

She had the gift and did not know it. All the research I had read on those born with the gift and no one to validate and help to nourish it along, speaks of the above isolation, emotional problems and battles with depression as being normal.

Pa use to say that the dark forces want those of us who are chosen to carry a high dose of the gift to enhance their powers. The dark forces use as their most powerful tool a thick, black cloak of depression. For this is the only darkness those forces are allowed to slip over those who walk in light without being invited.

Through her own pain, fears, and self-doubts she had somehow found the courage to reach out to me. I looked across the road at the house, and I know that there and then in the noon day sun I heard it laugh at me.

I ran into my house through the side door and bolted it behind me. Sinking to the floor there beside the door I cried. I cried for my Granny and Pa. I needed them. Oh, how I needed them.

I got Haas instead.

I don t know just how long I sat there on that kitchen floor praying and crying, but afternoons shadows had faded from the windows when I felt someone touch my hair. I looked up and there Haas sat at the kitchen table looking down at me.

"There's no need to cry my child. She is part of the circle."

"Sam?"

"She's your fourth cousin."

"But I don't have any relatives."

"Long ago my father had an older sister. She was ten years older than he, and she had a different father. Up until my Grandfather the gift in his line had been passed solely from mother to daughter. He was the first, perhaps, because his father had the gift. What was his sister's name? Kate. By the time my father was six, Kate had married and moved away to a community called Whispering Springs. In those days, that was a great distance to travel so Kate didn't visit often. But she did keep up with her brother, my Father, your great-grandfather.

"Kate went on to have two children a boy and a girl, and they were ten years apart in age as well. The boy didn't have any trace of the gift which brought Kate great comfort for she had been watching my Father's growth by way of her gift. Unfortunately Kate's son didn't have much else. After six years of schooling he never learned to read or write."

"You said Kate had a daughter?"

"Yes Aubrey. Now Aubrey had intelligence, for she was reading and writing before she was five. She also had the gift, but by this time Kate wasn't looking at it as a gift any longer but rather as a curse for she saw her brother John make a change.

"Aubrey's brother married but never had any children. In time Aubrey herself married in the shadows of Amelia's revenge and had two children of her own, both girls and both ten years apart. The girls themselves showed only the slightest traces of having the gift and Aubrey, who by this time referred to the gift as a shine, was relieved.

"Aubrey's daughters grew up and in time married, each were blessed with daughters. The oldest had five the youngest had three. Aubrey's two youngest granddaughters, born one year and one month apart--one to each daughter--were born with thick veils. Samantha was born the same day at the same time as you but in a hospital some thirty miles away from you.

"Samantha thinks she has it, and she's both afraid and fascinated by it. She's lived her whole life not more than 15 miles from you. She's passed my house everyday of her life, and she's being drawn to it like a moth to a flame."

"What of Aubrey's other granddaughter?"

"Not understanding her heritage, she's willingly has taken the gift over to evil. You must understand that by ignoring the gift, by not cultivating it, by hoping that it will somehow just go away, Aubrey and her mother Kate unwittingly left the door open for evil to step right in and the insanity to continue."

We looked at each other for the longest time. There was so much I wanted to know, needed to know. So much I knew that he hadn't told me. And by what Uncle Haas didn't say I knew what had happened to my Mama.

I understood without knowing. I knew without need for confirmation that Sam's family had intentionally mated in an effort to kill the gift out. I knew that my family had done just the opposite to preserve the gift.

At that moment I knew the gift and with it one's true destiny could be delayed, pushed down, but could never ever be denied its moment of showing.

At that instant I understood with total clarity the phrase I'd heard so often used to describe the gift, it is a blessing that comes loaded with curses.

Most important of all to me was that by the time Haas had left, I knew that Sam and I would have a second chance.

If it were true that I had been born old, at that moment I aged on par with the ancients and was weighted with the insight and wisdom of several life times.

I had wanted Easter Sunday to be the day the Father and I spent in the house, but the good Father couldn't get away from his duties that weekend so I chose the first weekend in April. Father Mike had wanted to go over to the house prior to that weekend and I refused to go in, so we compromised on just walking around the outside.

I followed him as he walked upon the wraparound porch; I felt many things but said nothing. I lagged in back of him as he peered through windows and touched the house here and there.

Neither of us spoke as we stepped off the porch in front of the side door. He walked onto the left going behind the house and I allowed myself to follow as if I were led. He stopped in front of the first root cellar with its field stone front and nice cottage windows and doors. It looked for all the world like a child's playhouse hollowed out of a hill.

I stood back as he stepped upon the small field stone walkway that led to the door. If only he'd taken two steps forward he would have been to the door. He took one step and hesitated then turned and continued walking off to the left.

From the back, the house looked huge and looming. Between its height and the forest of trees that stood on the hill just behind it, no sunlight ever hit its back, so a thick carpet of moss covered the ground that led to the second root cellar. This one had no cozy front, no windows, just a solid door that if opened would only lead to the dark bowels of the earth. I noticed that the padlock was rusting but still holding firm and for that I was grateful.

"Do you have this key Grace?"

"I have all of them."

"You should destroy this one."

Before I could reply we both heard and felt a low rumble. We looked at one another as if for an answer. Father Mike veered up the hill, and I quickly followed knowing at that moment that I could have never done this alone.

The sound and vibration stopped. We looked down at the top of the second root cellar. There was no moss growing on that well-packed dirt just a few stones here and there. The Father looked at me with a question in his eyes. I gave him the only answer I knew.

"Grass won't grow on a busy street."

Father Mike reached out and touched my arm. I looked to him then followed his gaze. There on the back wall of that white house, between the first and second story windows, written in blood red child's scrawl, were the words: go home priest.

I must admit that my first instinct was to run. But we both stood rooted as it were staring at the words, watching as they slowly faded.

When the words were completely gone, the Father and I continued our walk around the root cellar to the side of the house. I know now just as I knew then that I heard laughter.

About ten years after Uncle Haas had been locked away, both Granny and Pa had felt the need to go ahead and have this house wired and hooked to electricity when they had theirs done. It was then that she took her lawyer's advice and decided to go ahead and rent the house out to avoid its slow rotting. That was the first and one of the few times that I think my Granny tried to deny her heritage.

Quite a few years back, shortly after that self-proclaimed new age psychic fled the house late one night in terror, and the electric meter blew up. Supposedly it happened because lightening hit a transformer a couple of miles down the road. It was then that Granny made the decision not to have it replaced. As we rounded the house, I remembered that incident.

Father Mike stopped so quickly that I very nearly ran into him, I once again followed his gaze. For what seemed like the longest time we stood and watched as sparks danced around that circle where the meter had been hissing and snapping.

As one, we looked up over our heads, the black wire that led to the house from a power pole out by the roadside was alive with dancing--hissing humming sparks. Very slowly, we walked away hearing the sounds turn to whispered words that burned and seared their way to our very souls.

"Death awaits..."

"Death awaits..."

"Death awaits."

I've traveled the world over studying the gift and its many properties. I've participated in a number of studies, allowed my gifts to be tested and have been written up in the trades. I have both attended and participated in seminars, lectures, and argued in debates. I have written extensively about psychic healing and psychic properties in objects. Through my experiences, I have met many vast and wonderfully gifted personalities blessed with the gift, and what has always amazed and comforted me the most has been the sense of family connection among those who are truly gifted.

What makes me mention this here and now was the sudden appearance of my Texas Cowboy, just as the Father and I had crossed the road and stepped onto the porch of my home, Jesse roared into the driveway. He is considered an expert in the paranormal field. He calls himself a spirit chaser. He jumped from his car in his cowboy boots, hat and jeans claiming that a mutual friend of ours, Janie, had called him from Paris telling him that I was in desperate need of his services.

The truth is that up until that very moment I hadn't thought I would. However, I must confess that when I saw him I felt a great wave of relief wash over me. Over the next hour or so, Father Mike and I relayed our plans and what had happened to us just before his arrival. Jesse and Father Mike seemed to get along quite well, and Jesse agreed to stay and accompany us on Friday.

After Father Mike left, Jesse and I settled into a quiet one-on-one banter about destiny and whether or not one could alter destiny or change the inevitable. As usual he and I were on opposite sides of the fence.

Finally, Jesse arose and announced that he was going over before it got dark and take a look around. I cautioned him against doing it and watched as he went out the door.

From my chair by the window, I was able to watch him as he crossed the road. The only thought I had was a word. One word and that word screamed in my ear, "sacrifice!"

I jumped from the chair and ran like I had never run before. As I crossed the road, he was walking around the porch. I have heard people complain of not being able to yell or speak in a crisis. Well my voice was frozen, and my mind was only able to connect with the house, thus I saw what happened mere seconds before it happened, and my feet froze where they stood and I tried to pray.

In silent horror I watched Jesse move around the porch to the side door, and turn away from the house. He stood on the edge of the porch looking off into the woods as if he saw something. Then from the door, what I can only describe as a large hand of light reached out and shoved Jesse, sending him up and out a good twenty feet. He landed on the other side of the driveway.

Just as he landed, I found my voice and my feet. I remember the house laughing as I ran to Jesse knowing full well what I had to do. Jesse had broken his leg and sprained his back. He was kept in the hospital overnight for observation. I went to get him the next morning only to find out that he'd have to stay one more night. I was relieved but tried not to let it show.

Though he was disappointed at having to stay another night, he relayed to me his excitement over the fact that he'd still be able to get out in time to go with me and Father Mike on Friday. I told him that I thought maybe we should just beg off and rethink this thing through a little deeper. He felt that I was wrong and then told me to stay away from that place. I assured him that I would be just fine and then I left.

On the way home I stopped by the camping supply store and bought a dozen battery- powered lanterns and a cooler. I also stopped off at a small grocery store and bought some drinks and ice for the cooler.

I drove just passed my house and pulled into Haas and Matilda's driveway. Taking the key from the glove box, I walked up onto the porch and unlocked the side door and began to unload the car.

I walked around the high-ceilinged rooms of the first floor; my boots echoing on the burnt cherry hardwood floors. I wish I knew words that would adequately convey to you how I felt as that big old house wrapped itself around me.

I began my tasks by setting a lantern on the kitchen counter, another on the fireplace mantle in the living room and another on the fireplace mantle in Matilda's parlor. It wasn't until I started up the stairs with my arms loaded with lanterns that I began to feel weighed down. It was as if the air had become heavier. I sat a lantern down in the window sill at the top of the stairs and another in the window at the far end of the hall.

Slowly, I opened the first bedroom door and walked across the hardwood floors to the window and sat another lantern down on its sill taking the time to notice my home across the road. An overwhelming feeling of loneliness washed over me. Quickly, I turned and repeated my actions in the next two bedrooms.

I was standing in the fourth bedroom window just over the side door looking out into the woods when I saw something move. Despite an overwhelming urge to run, I stood my ground straining to get a better view. In time I saw it again; it was a shadow—a very distinct shadow.

I don't know just how long I stood there, but evening's first shadows had fallen across the room when I came to myself and looked down at my watch. Quickly, I lit the lantern there in front of me and raced through the rest of the upstairs rooms lighting lanterns.

I paused at the top of the steps debating the attic. I had intended to light it up as well, but right then and there I was filled with a deep foreboding sense of doom at the very thought of opening that little door and going up those dark narrow steps. I looked over my shoulder at the attic passage and cursed myself as I went down the stairs in front of me.

To say that I was filled with second thoughts at this point would be making light of all my feelings. I wanted only one thing right then and there and that was to get out of that house and run—run as far and as fast as I could. I wanted with every fiber in my being to forget about that crazy little word called destiny.

I had about an hour of daylight left so instead of running, I grabbed a can of soda from the cooler and went out onto the front porch.

As I sat there, I knew that here alone was how it was meant to be. It was a family circle that had been opened, and it was family only that could close it. I also knew that the only thing that could truly stop me was the fear that I would show by having someone by my side regardless of how qualified I felt they may have been. This was a family thing—a family problem that had been caused by fear, by ignorance, by not communicating, and most of all by hoping that time would heal all wounds and all indiscretions. Therefore, it was up to family to break the cycle and stand up to what family had birthed, no matter their beliefs, fears or reasons.

I got up and went in just before the last shadows of the evening fell across the yard. I went throughout the first floor of the house lighting the lanterns. When I finished I grabbed another can of soda and sat down in the middle of the living room floor.

I remember thinking just how much I liked this house with its large rooms that flowed one into the other, the old cherry hardwood floors gave the house a warmth that did nothing to bespeak of the terror that lay hidden here. It was obvious to even the most untrained of eyes just how much thought, planning, and craftsmanship had went into the building of this house. And it was this loving craftsmanship that made me wonder how many boards and nails were crafted in spells and dark solemn promises.

Just as the last of the day's shadows slipped from the sky and night's embrace had firmly wrapped its hold onto the house, I heard the breathing. Slowly, I got up and walked from room to room; the breathing continued no louder in one room than the next. It wasn't labored, but rather relaxed and just out of sequence with my own.

I stopped off in what had once been Matilda's parlor; I studied carefully the sweat glistening off the wall. I reached up and touched it. Despite the cool night that was in the house, the moisture was warm.

I looked around and suddenly the empty room was filled with what I knew instinctively to be Matilda's things—her velvet covered rocking chair was sitting next to the fireplace. An old victrola sat on a marble-topped tabled that had ball and claw feet. The sofa was lovely with its delicate wood trim, and the pink lace curtains strained to keep the night from overtaking the room. Carefully, I stepped over and touched the lace tatted doily that was laid across the back of Matilda's rocker and felt her soul touch my own. The feeling was one of the most awe-inspiring I've ever had.

In an instant, I saw her life played out in front of my mind's eye. I felt her feelings, listened to her whispered dreams, and knew as my own her fears and beliefs.

"Haas is at peace and waiting for you, Matilda," I whispered, as I felt her soul begin to move away from my own. I had tears in my eyes and chills up my spine when she materialized before me bathed in a brilliant white light. Her beauty took my breath away.

"I've been waiting for you, Grace. From these very windows I've watched you grow. All about you is as it should be."

"Why am I here Matilda?"

"To close the circle...to shatter the lies. "

"How?"

"You will know. It's up to you and yours alone to shatter these chains that hold me here—their promise fulfilled."

"How will I know what to do?"

"You have love in your heart, Grace. Your soul is filled with compassion; follow that compassion. Your mind is opened and filled with a wisdom and truth that reaches far beyond your years. Follow wisdom's truth. And most of all, trust what you know and do not put faith in the things that you do not know to be true."

Matilda turned as if looking behind her, "The hour is close at hand when he will appear. If you open your senses and trust in your first response, you will close the circle and begin for yourself a new destiny filled with new beginnings. If you hesitate, if you question anything that happens here tonight, the circle will shatter unclosed and open for you a destiny where all your beginnings will become ends and all hope for all members of this line will be lost for all times. Do not be afraid. He feeds on fear."

Before I could speak, she was gone. Her room was empty and sadness enveloped me.

As I stood there in my sadness, I heard the sound of shattering glass. Quickly, I turned and left the room. As I came from the parlor and stood beside the staircase I heard muffled laughter and the sound of bare feet padding across the hardwood floors upstairs.

As I debated with myself the merits of climbing the stairs, I heard the sound of breaking glass again. This time, I realized that the sound was coming from outside. I stepped forward to the glass door and saw...

Looking back, I can say that I was scared; at the time I didn't feel fear. I only stood there watching what might have come straight from the pen of a third- rate horror writer. I tried very briefly to tell myself that all those very nearly transparent spirits—for lack of a better phrase—were in my mind. They couldn't be real. Couldn't be.

Then I heard Matilda's voice, "Trust your first response."

Okay, they were real. I continued watching as the front and side yards became filled with those aberrations. Then, I heard the distinct creaking sound of a door on rusted hinges being opened. With a third eye I never knew I had until that moment, I watched as a man of incredible beauty step from the root cellar that so resembled a child's playhouse. I knew that if I ran to the back of the house, I wouldn't be able to see him any more clearly than I was seeing him right then.

As I followed his movements to the side of the house, I was aware of cars passing by on the highway out front. The house was lit up and at least a hundred of those glowing spirits filled the front yard alone and more stepped slowly from the woods. But no one seemed to notice. No one slowed down. Couldn't they see them?

"Of course not," Haas whispered.

The beautiful man was now just past the side door, still walking in the yard. He was going to come around to the front; I knew that even before it became obvious. I realized that I could read his intentions, at least for brief instances.

As he rounded the corner and stood in front of the house surrounded by what I knew were his people, I saw him clearly with my actual vision. His image was crisp and clear; there were no flaws or distortions about him.

He was tall—very tall, his raven black hair shimmered hints of blue in the pale moonlight and looked to be as soft as feathers. I doubt I'll ever see another man with more well-chiseled features, and a better sculptured body. I think that he held in his entire being the beauty of the Greek gods that mythologists write about.

He was in direct contrast to his people, all of whom seemed distorted in their features. They filled the yard in long white-hooded robes; he stood there in a black garb that stretched taut across his muscular frame. He lifted his face and looked directly at me. His coloring was pale, and his blood red eyes attempted to bore through to my soul.

I had no instinct, no first response. As he stepped up onto the porch, I stepped back. I looked down at his feet as I heard the sound he made stepping onto the wooden porch.

His feet were hoofed, like that of a goat. I took two more steps back as he stepped through the door.

Nothing broke, the door was not opened. He simply materialized through it as if it weren't there at all.

"I've been waiting for you, Grace. Your Mama promised you to me."

His voice was incredibly lyrical, enchanting if you will. I shook my head; "You're not entitled to me."

"You are mine!"

"Only if I had been brought to you before the age of twelve, or had called you out and asked you to accept me."

"You played at my feet. I watched you all these years. I called to you. You are mine!"

He stepped forward. I stepped back. "I have come here in light."

"You came in ignorance at my bidding."

"I came in the white light of the Holy Spirit's destiny."

"Piss your light!" he roared.

With the wave of his hands, the lanterns went dark throughout the house. The house was now in shadows. I heard his people begin to chant, "Come into the dark. Hail the prince of night."

With all my thoughts, with all my energy, with a power I didn't know I possessed I yelled, "NO! You come into the LIGHT!" The lanterns all through the house came back on. He took one step back. It was only one step but to me, at that moment, it was the world.

Until... the chants lowered and became words wrapped in a language I was not at all familiar with. His eyes glowed redder, almost pulsating with intensity, and then I heard a rumbling—low at first, and then the floor began to shake.

The lantern behind me on the mantle fell to the floor and went dark. One by one, I heard lanterns fall onto hard wood floors throughout the house, as room by room fell victim to the darkness.

As he and I stood there facing one another bathed only in the pale moonlight and the waning lights cast by the security lights across the road, I became angry. And as this was my first response, I felt I could trust in it.

The rumbles had stopped, neither of us had moved. I felt I had the advantage for his eyes glowed red so I could stare into them, even in the dark. My anger grew because of what I saw there in his eyes.

I saw fire, people withering and crying out in the pain of a sacred trust violated; their screams of agony—the agony that comes from being burned in a fire that does not consume.

Then I saw abandoned houses, hospitals, schools, hotels, post offices scattered the world over. I saw before me buildings without number where I knew he and his lay waiting like serpents; just waiting to strike.

Deep inside myself, I felt my anger begin to boil. I became aware of it and worked feverishly to keep that awareness pure and that anger of the holiest white light I could envision. For I knew and I will share with you here a truth about anger, it is the one emotion that is the greatest spiritual tool out there. If the anger is one of pure white love and mercy, it can move mountains and save souls; if it is one of self righteousness or fear—even hate, then it can level mountains and destroy souls. And the souls it saves or destroys begin with the person holding the anger in their heart.

I heard his hoofs take a step on the floor.

"You will take me in light if you take me at all."

He laughed, and his laughter helped my anger become all consuming. I saw in his eyes a seductive presence that lured beautiful girls and desperate weakened men to do his bidding, only to be destroyed in the false hopes of promises he made but would not keep even if he'd had the power to keep them.

Suddenly, the overhead light flickered. It was only a flicker, but it hushed his viscous laughter.

What I saw in his eyes next was meant to scare me, but it only served to fortify my anger. And that anger became such that it literally made me see flashes of color. When I heard his hoofs approach me, I did not move. I stood firm and thought only of light.

Light, that great beacon of security that chases monsters from closets and keeps wild beast of prey away. Light! Light!

Just as he reached out to touch me, all through the house the overhead lights came on. I heard the creatures outside in white shriek as the porch lights also came on. And determined as he was, he allowed his own anger to surface and stepped forward with his arms outstretched to me.

It was just as I reached to push his evil hands from me that with that third sight I saw her beat up brown station wagon pull into the yard with its bright lights glaring, sending the army of his servants shrinking back, with their white robed arms over their faces.

His strength was so great, that there was no way I could have won the fight alone, and his touch—his fingers burned a cold that was as hot as fire around my throat. I knew no fear. I realized that he was unaware of Sam's approach. The lights flickered and I focused not on the intense pain I felt, but on light.

Light was my only instinct. Despite watching Sam with my third sight, I thought only of Jesus and his precious light. I refused and denied the thing before me entrance into my mind even though I knew the pain would stop if I did.

Sam stumbled from the car crying; she was very nearly hysterical. She ran around the front of the car and ran up the steps falling onto the front porch. With tears streaming down her face and her body shaking, she pulled herself up and stumbled on through the front door.

"LET HER GO!"

Her voice filled the room with so much power and surety that he did just that and turned to her laughing. It was such a menacing laugh that a sick fear couldn't help but spread up from the pit of my stomach and wash over my body. For a brief moment, I felt weakness try to attack my knees.

"YOU!" he roared, "Look at you. For thirty years I've beckoned to you, haunted your dreams, hung around you clawing at the edges of your pathetic little soul."

I cringed at his words and flippant tone; for I was looking at a girl. She may have been thirty-two but with her tear swollen cosmetic-free face and long brown disheveled hair, she looked, for all the world, like a little girl lost and alone as she stood there in the door. I remember thinking this is my white knight?

"Look at you, big brave man of hell. You're not as strong as you think if you couldn't get past the edges of my pathetic little soul! And now you think that you can hurt me with your words? You think you can make me bow before you because you speak the truth? If you want my fear you're gonna have to tell me more than I already know." Sam's voice was so void and dead of emotion that it sent chills up my spine.

"You're here. It's gonna be a better night for me and my kingdom than I had planned."

"You and your kingdom be damned!" I was shocked by the level of contempt in Sam's voice. "Your little kingdom is nothing but more of the pain and loneliness that my life has been. Your evil is sick. You're sick. I'm sick. You want someone for your little kingdom? Then take me. Take me and leave Grace. I have nothing, as you so eloquently pointed out; nothing to lose by stopping you."

"NO! Sam, I can..."

He turned and looked at me. His look silenced my words and my mind. The lights flickered and his eyes pulsated a blinding flash of red. I thought lights. I called on Granny and Pa and thought lights.

He turned back to her as the lights came back on. They were dim, but they were on.

"You can't stop me little girl. But I'll take you first." He stepped toward her, a sinister chuckle emitting from his throat. The lights flickered once more.

To my surprise and utter horror she stepped forward to him a willing victim, her arms hanging limply at her side. I screamed for Haas as I watched this hooven entity wrap his long talon-like fingers around her throat.

The lights flickered again.

Tears silent, silent and hot tears streamed down my face.

For just a moment, I allowed the lights to go off.

In that moment, I had forgotten Matilda's warning. It was in the darkest hollow of my soul that I heard a scream—a man's scream—a scream that shook the very foundation of that big old house. It was a scream that sounded like thousands of mice caught roasting in a barn fire, and it echoed across all time and eternity.

I looked up and saw him backing away from her. Slightly bent, this beautiful man creature was screaming in a torment of the ages. He looked at me with eyes that were no longer red but rather pink; it was then that I saw the origin of his pain. Burned into his forehead, at that place of the third eye, was a small image of a crucifix, and from his temples were what I could only describe as small horns were emerging. For the briefest of moments, I felt pity for him as very slowly he faded into nothingness, amid pure black putrid smoke that was the sum total of all the promises he represented. When he was gone, the overhead lights flickered on and I looked at Sam who was standing by the door with her head down and her shoulders sagging. I crossed the distance and took her into my arms.

I felt her tense after a few moments, and then I heard her voice. "Who are they?"

I pulled away from her and looked behind me. I finally felt total peace. Through tears I smiled and introduced my cousin Sam to Haas and his lovely wife Matilda, as well as my Granny and Pa.

God never takes what he doesn't replace.

Time is a healer. And Sam is healing. The depression and misfortune that hung over her all her life is slowly lifting. She is an exceptional student and is continually amazed at the powers she has.

Her daughter has become the light of my life and I teach her as well. She shows remarkable promise.

My own destiny of dreams is beginning to take shape as Jesse and I find new levels in our friendship. We're looking forward to a Christmas wedding in 1996.

That big old house is free now. And just as Hass and Matilda requested I have given it to Sam and her husband. They are busy rediscovering one another and the love they almost lost as they renovate that house making Haas' dream a reality, by turning it into a home.

I have come to believe that the reason my Mama was not there the night the circle was closed was because she'd went to him and his darkness. Jesse agrees, and that realization leaves me cold. As I said earlier I could find out—I could know for sure, just by going to the attic and opening her trunk. But evil is best left alone once it's been banished, once the circle closes.

Prologue (3)

Unfortunately Sam and her husband's time on earth was cut tragically short. And so it was that after just three years of rediscovering one another, they parted ways. And Sam? Well as some of you no doubt know she went on to become an ordained minister of Gnosis and a wildly successful author and lecturer teaching the livable spiritual concepts that she has come to know.

Her daughter has her gifts and unlike her mother she has grown up knowing about them and how to use them. Myself and Jesse have made sure of that and rarely has there been one more talented and more powerfully gifted.

Jesse and I went on to get married and we are still holding on to one another and have had our hands full raising our identical triplet daughters, Leela Rose, Lily Iris, and Lila Daisy; born one year to the day after our wedding. Then seven years to the day later, we were blessed with the appearance of our son, Lance Forrest. All our children are gifted and run the gambit of gifts and abilities. They have been mine and Jesse's priority and have been the brightest light to shine in my grandparents' home since they chose to leave this earth.

As you may have noticed I wrote the stories of my family some 12 years ago and laid them back. I had felt that it was important to preserve, for my children the stories and memories that rooted and completed their family's legacy, just as I had received and reflected on them. Back then I had no intention of ever publishing them.

Then a few years ago, I felt the urge to trace the member of my family that went off to live in Whispering Springs. As one thing was leading to another, my publisher called and as we made small talk she said that I should write an autobiography and I mentioned that I had written some short stories that told of my experiences and my family's legacy, and she asked to read them so I sent them on. After reading them, she suggested that I turn them into a book. But I am a stubborn and rather temperamental writer. I said that they should be maintained as a trilogy for each story spoke of facts and insights that both contributed to the events that unfolded and would be lost to sacrifice if converted to a traditional book format. She said as long as I could make them appear to be a book then she would consider it. So, if you are reading this and you are not a member of my family or a close personal friend then you know that in between children, home schooling lessons, lectures, and other obligations of the gift, I pulled what I was told was the impossible, off.

It was about this time, that I met a young woman from Whispering Springs, Lindsey, Whimsy's great-granddaughter. She shared with me the transcript that follows. Since it makes mention of my family and talks about even more of the unknowingly gifted people, and I would even daresay the places in Cedars County, I wanted to share it with you. And so it is with her permission that I publish it here. A more appropriate ending to this wonderful heirloom collection, I could not have planned nor envisioned.

WHISPERING SPRINGS

I'm sitting here on the front porch of the trailer home that my son went out and bought me when the kitchen floor in my house went and fell through. I don't reckon he expected me to live so long, I know I didn't. I'll be a hundred and one in a couple of days.

I use to sit on the porch of the old place behind here, because I like porch sitting on nice days. That's why my son went and built me a porch on this here tin house. He said the old place wasn't a fit to even be around. But I won t let him go and tear the old place down neither. Cause there's been enough tearing down around these parts in the last ninety-eight years. I figure that when I die, I'll blow it down on my way up to heaven, or I'll pull it down with me when I go to the other place if I ain't been quite good enough to go up.

Ninety-eight years is how long I a-member. There are heaps and piles of memories in my mind. That's why I like porch sitting; it gives me plenty of remembering time.

I live in Whispering Springs. Of course it ain't called that no more. It ain't been called that since the federal government went and closed up the post office just down the road, a few years after the Second World War. No, where I live, ain't called nothing no more.

I look around me at all this here land and them new brick houses scattered here and there, and I can't hardly believe this use to be a bustling little town of sorts. Least ways when I was a growing up that's what the farm kids called me, town folk, a cause our house, the one out back of here, was right here kindly in the middle of it all.

My driveway over yonder used to be the road that led to the tavern with rooms to let overhead and the old saw mill, and the area's biggest graveyard. And that road there that runs a-front of my house here used to lead to the post office, general store, gristmill, and between here and there was some other businesses.

Let me see now: there was a leather tanner, a barber shop, the old school, a blacksmith. The only business that still stands—though just barely—is the old post office and the gristmill that was next to it.

The post office, speaking of it, reminds me that in this here trailer house of mine I got me a couple of old boot boxes crammed with letters and postcards marked Whispering Springs. I guess that's about the only proof there is left that this here was once a place with a name.

Progress, it done came and knocked down the whole lot of my past, making me a doubt my memories sometimes. It's easy to doubt your memories when you get to be as old as me. Then again, sometimes the past, it comes back so strong that it comes pretty nigh on a knocking me down.

That's why I porch sit, and on ugly days I window sits.

A couple a weeks back I had my grandson drive me over there to what used to be called Spirit Springs and it done went away like this place. Only things left there is the old general store and it's all boarded up, and them there seers place, why that old house still stands a testament of some sort.

John and Martha was their name, though I can't quite a-member their last names. They had a son and twin daughters, terrible what happened to them girls. Then their son Haas, he went mad and kilt his pretty young wife, the killing, it drove him mad, and his place still stands. I noticed that they was some people a fixing it up a might. That did my old heart a bit of good.

Old John's sister, she lived here in Whispering Springs, as did her children and most of her children's children. No one much knew that but its true none the less.

No-sir-ree-bob it don't help me out too awful much to see how these little places just went and dried up with nary even a marker to say that they ever was. That us people who lived, loved, worshiped and buried our dead in an, oft time hand to mouth way, never were.

It's for the sickness in my heart that I feel when I realize how all this progress has forgotten us and our towns that I'm a sitting here on my porch a talking into this here contraption that my great grand-daughter gave me.

She's a sweet thing. She's wanting me to talk into this thing about the memories I live with every day. She's in college and has some crazy idea about preserving my past.

I told her I would a cause it's downright shameful the way the government folk took away my town just like it never were and left me pretty nigh on the only one who a members when this here place had a name. They could a at least put up a sign as to what once was.

I guess it bothers me a cause of my age. I did me a century of living, 98 years of it, right here on this very piece of land. I done seen and read it all. Even seen a murdered man not too awful far from this very porch. And it's hard to believe that when the good Lord calls me home I'll just leave and it'll be like I too never was. And all them beans I planted and canned, books I read, clothes I washed, what good was they if nobody a members, if it's like I never was. So, I'll talk into this here thing so that maybe a century of being won't be for naught.

I have me five older brothers, or should I say had, a cause they's all down where the tavern use to be a pushing up daisies and earthworms.

The tavern was torn down not long after the murder what happened not far from my porch. It was a rough place. But it was torn down, and the cemetery just kind of grew to take over its site. They's over 300 souls laid to rest there back there. But hardly anybody visits them. It's too far out of the way for folks now days.

Funny ain't it? People got cars to take 'em places in minutes that used to take us hours to go, but places are too far out of their way. They got machines to do their dishes, a figuring, planting, and clothes washing but they ain't got no time for a visiting, or a raising their children. Why I could laugh all day at that irony, if it weren't so sad.

But like I was a saying my name's Whimsy, and I was born the youngest. I got, or rather had me five big brothers. My Momma was sick from the day I was born right on up until she died when I was a nearing my fifteenth birthday. She didn't leave the bed much at all.

My Daddy won this place and two hundred acres out in the back in a poker bet. (He never played poker again). Then we came to live here when I was just three. All I got left of the place now is about twenty acres right around this here home site. Time sure do takes its toll don't it?

We came to live here in the house out back in 1901. Oh my, they's so many memories a flooding me. They all want to come out at once. It's almost like they's afraid that if they don't speak first they'll all be lost forever. This floods a coming nigh on a taking my breath away.

My first memory is the day we moved here. The biggest reason we moved here aside from the fact that my Daddy won it, and it was a bit closer to his Daddy's place, was a so that Momma would be closer to the doctor, and the good church ladies who helped Momma set up the house and then run it until I was trained. And my training started that very day.

I didn't have me much of a childhood, didn't get me too much schooling back then either, that came later. But I made the most of every opportunity what came my way all my life.

By the time I was five I was a cooking on that big wood cook stove that is now a sitting on the ground of what use to be the kitchen floor in the house out back. I had to do my cooking a standing on a wood stool my Daddy built just for that reason.

I made the morning breakfast, and by seven I was a gathering the eggs, milking the cow, churning butter on the butter days, and in the right seasons I planted and tended a little garden out back of the house.

By the time I was 10 year old, I could run the house just as well as any adult woman.

My Momma taught me to sew, embroider, crochet, and knit. Those are my Momma memories. When I had the housework settled down I'd sit on Momma's bed and she'd tell me stories of how it was, and how she wished it could be. As we sewed or broke beans, shelled peas, or peeled apples for sun drying she'd teach me her beliefs about God, love, men, marriage, and a woman's strengths and woes.

Momma was ahead of her time with her woman thinking. She said that sooner or later the men folk would lose out and show their true laziness. Then like always, the women folk would step in and pick up the slack like they always had. It was her opinion that within the next two hundred years the women would be a working outside the home as well as inside and a raisin' their children alone, since the men folk she knew of did little else with the children aside from a whipping them in line.

Momma would have been surprised to see that it took less than a hundred years for some of her predictions to unfold. I've often wondered what Daddy did to make my Momma so bitter about men. But then again a woman's life was work seven days a week from sunup to sunset. Idle hands would make a poor woman a harlot. I heard that a lot back then.

So maybe Momma's bitterness was something that she came by honest like. Times in her day and place were so hard that if a person didn't come by things real honest like that, they were usually hanged on the wrong side of the law.

My Daddy, he and the boys was always out a working. They raised cattle, trained mules, grew tobacco and feed corn, built houses and barns, made furniture, and cut up firewood. I saw little of them.

But Daddy always took notice and complimented my cooking and housework. And it was he that taught me my woodworking skills. The times I spent with him weren't much but they was times of talking past instructions. Daddy was a tall man, not at all prone to hugging or spoiling. But he was always kind to me.

I liked my Daddy. Men like him were and still to this day are a rare lot. I always knew exactly where I stood with him as did anyone who met him. He gave everyone the benefit of the doubt upon a meeting them and extended heaps of respect whether they kept that respect or lost it was up to them. But once you lost my Daddy's respect you never got it back.

It was my Daddy who would take us out past the tavern on the hill on silent Sundays, on out past the sawmill closed for a day's rest, to the cemetery. Where the view was and is still something that takes my breath away, beautiful and the quiet stillness was and is such that it roars in the head and fills you with the power and peace of God.

Once there, we would visit with all the names on the rocks and in hushed tones befitting the reverence of God's own cathedral, Daddy would tell me stories about the people lying under the names.

I guess that was his way of making all that they was and did last for one more generation.

John Houston settled in these parts around 1730, he died and was the first one laid to rest that big cemetery. He'd brought with him his wife and about a dozen or so young ones as well as long time friends, Robert and Mayzell Harding who were born1710 and 1715 respectively and died together in a house fire in the winter of 1762.

Then there are stones that stood and stand in testament of the scarlet fever epidemic what claimed fifty lives in 1825, the blue babies born dead, the first, second and third wives that died in child bearing.

Then we'd come to a big stone that said in memory of Zekial Farley. That's all it said and still says. I'd ask if he was lying under it and Daddy'd always say no, and then I'd ask why and Daddy would answer, because evil people never truly die.

Now I'm a curious sort and always have been. I guess being curious just comes natural when you grow up in a place called Whispering Springs. So by the time I was twenty I had learned me a lot about Old Zekial Farley. Despite the fact that no one ever wanted to talk about him. I've found that what people don't want to talk about is quite often the very things they can't wait for a captive audience to tell it to.

They say that Zekial Farley stood seven and a half feet tall and lived to be a hundred years old. Of course back in his day rumor was spread that he'd never actually been born but rather came into being about a thousand years before his reign of terror.

Legends are always placed into perspective through records though. And the records at the county show that he was born to Lansford and Cordellia Farley in 1799. There's no record of his death, or for that matter of his parents' death and no real memory of what became of them. Much less where they came from though some rumors say that Lansford Farley came from the mountains of East Tennessee and that Cordellia was somehow related to them seers over to Spirit Springs. A place that, according to pure rumor, got its name a cause of the powers of that seer family that it seemed always did and do still live over by that way.

Now Zekial was said to have sold his soul to the devil on his thirteenth birthday. Up in that there juniper grove, that is just up the hill about a half mile down that there road out in the front of my house. And a boy who had always been known for his terrorizing pranks became downright sadistic.

The town folk were grateful for the relative peace when he'd disappear into that juniper grove for days on end. But when he came out they say that he was all wild-eyed and blood hungry. Legend has it that he ate his chickens raw and unplucked, biting their heads off first.

It is for sure that he took what he wanted when the mood struck him to take it, and if anyone dared try and stop him it was said that he would cut loose a yelling out for all to hear the dirty little secrets, thoughts and desires that were buried in the hearts of his victims. A causing them to shrink away in shame and let him have his way, just a so he'd quiet down.

Funny how the first two places built in these parts outside of houses and barns was a tavern and a church. And they were built in that order.

Now Zekial ran from the church building like the devil himself and took to the tavern like a duckling takes to a pond. There in the tavern he made his drinking stakes playing poker and extorting cash to keep his mouth closed. He caused fights, joined fights, and ended them as well. They say he had a hair trigger temper especially when he was a drinking the lightening water that old Homer Somsby or them Robinsons from over in Bored Valley was said to have made.

It is said that within his life time Zekial Farley killed at least a dozen people and dumped their bodies in the bogs a mile or so out back of the tavern. Old Zekial is also known to have borrowed horses without asking and burnt down more than one barn.

Finally, in 1850 it's said that the men folk of the township grew tired and reasoned that if they banded together they could bring an end to his tyranny. So they picked up their rifles and walked into that juniper grove.

It's said that the men folk lost their resolve when they found the place that Zekial was a worshipping at. There he stood in front of a pile of stones a small fire built in it, buck naked covered in soot. When he turned and saw them some fifty feet, more or less, away his normally ice blue eyes glowed red and he is said to have raised hands into the air a causing two massive trees to fall.

The men folk turned tail and ran for all they were worth and Old Zekial reigned on in terror for almost another decade.

Then Old Zekial went too far.

It was right afore the civil war broke out somewhere around the end of 1859 when old Zekial Farley felt a stirring and raped the tavern keeper's wife. It's said that he beat her to within an inch of her life. It is also rumored that the tavern keeper himself old Buzz Halfacre did the beating or at least the worst part of it.

It's well known that old Buzz had said afterward that Old Zekial should have made him kill her, cause now after being violated by the likes of Zekial Farley she was worthless.

Her name was Zeta, and after that night she starved herself in a miserable lonely hell. For her husband turned his back on her and the womenfolk of the township afraid of facing their own worse fears in her eyes shunned her. Zeta Dae Hoover Halfacre died about six months later. No one came to her funeral as there wasn't any and she lays resting about a hundred feet from old Buzz in the cemetery out back.

Finishing with Zeta hadn't been the end of Zekial's merry making that night. If it had then the odds are good that Old Zekial would have continued on in his ways for who knows how much longer. Instead he was just getting started when he left Zeta still undiscovered in her shame.

Angry and filled with the hate of the damned he went across to the sawmill and set it ablaze and just kept right on a stumbling, yelling, and a cursing the town folk's God, and all their two-faced piety.

He eventually came upon the Hanson's chicken coop and set about tearin' the chickens in it apart. Now old man Hanson had been down at the tavern and was now a part of the bucket brigade at the sawmill, and no one had yet thought to run down and ring the town bell to call out more reinforcements for that bucket brigade or else maybe, just maybe Zekial would have ended with the chickens.

As it was, while his father was sobering up passing along buckets of water down at the sawmill fire, Tomas Hanson, home alone, as his mother had died some two years back of consumption, was awaken to the sound of the chickens squawking for their lives and his dog growling from a place within his throat Tomas had never heard him growl before. So he grabbed up his Pa's gun and set out to kill himself a fox.

Well as you now know it were no fox in the chicken coop. So when young Tomas confronted a tall man covered in blood and soot, he hesitated firing his weapon. And while no one will ever know for sure what happened next everyone knew what the end results were. Tomas Hanson and his dog lay their necks broken in a bloody chicken coop surrounded by dead chickens their heads separated from their bodies.

Then just as suddenly as Old Zekial had started, in his reign of terror, he called it quits. Perhaps he'd had his fill of blood and flames for the night. No one will ever know why, but he was seen running from the Hanson place yelling as if being chased by the devil himself into his juniper grove.

By the time the fire was out, the shame found out, the cruelty exposed, and the dollars and cents of Zekial's path of rampage added up; it was almost noon on the third Saturday in October. The men folk were livid. The fear for their women and children scared them a little more than the memory of a crazed figure making trees fall. So they gathered together and prepared for what they considered a holy battle. Assembling the weapons old wives tales deemed necessary. They would after all be battling a demon.

Silver coins were melted down into bullets the drippings molded into pellets for slingshots. They fashioned arrows from white birch branches.

Their women gathered rats vein and brewed strong tea to give their men strength, they also gathered a mixture of mint leaves, citronella weed, and lemongrass for their men to rub over their bodies. The lemon was to open their eyes to the purity of evil, the mint to seal their souls to the oneness of God, and the citronella to repel the flies of Satan's beasts said to bite the unsuspecting and to plant seeds of vile thoughts. The preachers anointed the men with olive oil and put a clove of garlic in their left breast pockets.

The men gathered up their weapons and went into the juniper grove toward their own holy war. It was just a fore sundown.

As holy wars go, it weren't much. There was no lightening strikes no mighty hand of God came down from the sky. Though that would make for a more powerful ending wouldn't it?

No, all that happened was a bunch of rightfully scared and angry men went into a juniper grove and ended the terror of a mad man.

I almost feel sorry for Old Zekial Farley kneeling there in front of a pile of rocks covered in chicken blood and soot crying his heart out. I think he was truly repentant of his actions and sorry for what he was.

But these men were angry men, and as I said before, scared men and they saw their chance kneeling in front of them and took it opening fire with their weapons. I doubt they really noticed or cared that Zekial had his back to them. I believe that Zekial Farley died there that day at the age of 50.

Now I know that you're a memberin' how I said that he lived to be a hundred. But I hope you're also a memberin' how I said that there was no record of his death ever recorded.

The men folk never stepped forward and checked his body, he was never buried and he was left lying where he fell. When the men saw no movement from his body they left the sad grove.

A few days later they all went back and put a split rail fence around the grove declaring the grove off limits forever and a day.

A week later a horrible lightening storm came upon the town. They say that ball lightening ran along the fence and huge bolts struck a few of the trees in Old Zekial's grove. That's when a few of the town folk took to declaring that Zekial Farley still lived.

A few weeks after the lightening storm, just across the road there in front of my house down a little ways into that field the ground opened up and swallowed the New Baptist church. The church had looked out onto Zekial's grove and was the point of departure for the men as they set out to end the terror.

When the ground swallowed up the church is when everyone started to bolt their doors and windows again. A cause they all took to believing that Zekial was still alive.

Funny thing is that a Juniper tree now grows up out of that sink hole that ate the church.

Then everyday things like foxes in a hen house, snakes in the corn, pies missing from window sills, broken melons in fields, you name it, it was a blamed on poor Old Zekial, and offered up as proof that he didn't die.

Then the civil war came along and for folks around these parts that war made little sense. Families and friends went divided in their sympathies.

Now, no one around these owned any darkies except for Kaleb Finley, and by the time the war rolled around he'd sold them off as well as his other luxuries to cover the gambling debts that the loss of his ten thousand acres hadn't covered. No sir re, by the time the war came along he'd taken off out of these parts to never be heard from again; leaving a hundred acres more or less, the only truly stately home in all of Whispering Springs and seven sons to try and figure out how to settle up the remaining IOU's he'd left some rather greedy and spiteful people holding.

Now there's a story I'm a gonna try and remind myself to tell you later.

Anyways like I was a saying the town was divided. None of em could comprehend being rich enough to afford a slave. A sides they was a getting along just fine having a passel of kids and working long hard days of honest labor. After all, what good was money when it corrupted a man like Kaleb and to a lesser extent old Buzz Halfacre.

Then there was the other side of the coin, the side what really divided them. How could a government so far away tell them what they could and couldn't do, and how to do it? Especially a government many of them felt didn't fairly represent them and had no idea at all how they lived.

Remember that back in them days of horse and buggies Washington was as far away as the moon, especially in Whispering Springs where the nearest rail line was a half day away by horse and buggy.

So, folks in places like Whispering Springs had no more comprehension of city life than those city folk had of the back breaking, nature dependant life of back wood country folk.

The rest of the argument was how could a man born in Kentucky a place where; to this day many southern folks is divided about whether it is part of the north or the south, was at that time considered a part of the south, possibly turn his back on his own people.

But the free-thinkers in Whispering Springs looked at all the same arguments and felt that Lincoln, one of their own, who was a good and smart Christian man with southern roots, was right. Of course they did judge the moral fiber of wealthy land owners by Kaleb Finley.

Eventually the war that missed Spirit Springs some thirty miles away marched right through Whispering Springs and for five long years Old Zekial Farley was allowed to rest. A cause now, lost live stock and crops were rightfully blamed on soldiers both Yankee and Confederate alike.

And while the young men of Spirit Springs stayed home. By and large the young men of Whispering Springs filled their eyes with stars, their hearts with wonder-lust, and their bellies with venom, then took up guns and joined sides.

My Grand-Daddy who was up near thirty at the time told me he figured the troops marched through here partly a cause of the tavern and all the fresh water springs and caves. He also figured that the war started to come undone on the south's side with the appearance of the raiders like Camp Ferguson, who grew up about twenty miles from here as the crow flies, and his merry bunch of men.

The raiders were southern one and all and they fought for whichever side paid the most. And when they weren't a fighting they were out to plunder and pillage the helpless civilians. Sometimes when I study on all this I wonder if them seers over in Spirit Springs isn't what kept old Camp and his men not to mention the war away from their community.

What I do know is that it was a cause of them raiders that Roy Ray Pearson was killed not more than a mile from this very front door and his death was a tragic one. Sort a cause he was one of the bright sons from around these parts.

Old man Pearson married his first cousin and they had seven sons. Four were outright dim witted; one was just slow and loved to drink; two were as smart as the average man. But only one, Roy Ray had a kind heart and was slow to anger.

It was pretty nigh on close to the end of the war, long about the spring of 1864; and Roy Ray, who'd done his fighting for the North had come home on account of a missing arm and a leg wound that left him with a limp. He was up in his family's upper pasture where they kept what was left of their goats a checking on the pregnant mamma to see if he ought to bring her down to the barn yet. When through the woods he heard a powerful thundering of hoofs. Well he got up onto the back of his old mule and headed off for home. Well one thing about mules is that they ain't exactly known for their speed and racing endurance. Especially mules past ten years old.

About five hundred feet from his front door the mule dropped right out from under him and there beside his dead mule Roy Ray Pearson passed on over to the other side from a terrible case of lead poisoning. His family put up a marker right there on the site where he fell; a telling the day, time, and year of their fallen son's passing.

If I was able to I'd walk on down the road and get that information down for you. But at a hundred walking a mile there and a mile back is asking a lot. To this day the monument still stands in a patch of woods not more than forty feet from the road.

Like all things bad, the war came to an end, Old Camp Ferguson and his merry making men were tried for their war crimes and ole Camp was hanged and lays resting just across the way there not more than twenty miles, as the crow flies, from my back door. As if the war weren't bad enough the carpet beggars descended. None of them stayed around these parts long when they saw nary a rich man or house around. I also suspect that more than one met his end down in the bogs.

The folks around these parts were hard working and honest people. You didn't threaten to take what they had worked and endured so much to have, and have them take your threats lightly.

No sir, back then; why even in my day, a stranger didn't come into town and make threats. Especially not in a place filled plum to the brim with caves, bogs, hot springs, mud springs and sink holes. Why that threatening stranger just might find himself taking a walk he wouldn't be a coming back from.

Yep, around these parts the only fear the men folk had was in that hellfire and damnation God the preachers preached about on Sundays. After all these men all figured they had faced down the devil himself when they faced down Old Zekial Farley. So taking a stranger for a walk weren't nothing to them.

Whispering Springs had a reputation for being a rough sort of place. Of course its reputation was nothing like a little rail town about thirty miles, as the crow flies, from here that got the nickname of the Bloody Ten, because for the town and two miles on all four sides of it a body wasn't safe day or night. Unless of course you were born and raised there. Of course even then you watched out for you and yours, and walked clean around certain people and places.

Of course the biggest difference a twixt Whispering Springs and The Bloody Ten is that our reputation started to drop away with the depression years and The Bloody Ten's reputation continued on until about ten years back. But even now there's places around those parts no self-respecting or self-preserving local would go for love or money.

But here, here's so quiet with forgotten memories that it makes a body's ears hurt and heart ache.

I didn't want to live this long, not really, especially not if I'd known that I'd outlive my town. I look at the breezes blow thru the fields swaying the waist high hay, that's just about ready for cutting, and I remember the fall festivals of my youth. Somewhere far off I hear the hum of a chainsaw and it reminds me of the men coming up from the sawmill after a hard day's work, and of the wagons of logs that went down the road and the wagons of lumber what came up it.

The saddest part is I know I'm the only thing to a test for the lives that were. And that knowledge makes me scared to die. It makes me think that the whole point of living is well, somehow pointless. Especially if after we pass it's like we never were to begin with.

Listen to me wondering off from what I was a saying. I sound like a forgetful old lady and I ain't the least bit forgetful. And if I were to say that I had a problem it would be that I can't forget.

Like I was a saying before I so rudely interrupted myself. I reckon that Whispering Springs got its reputation a cause of the tavern.

After the Civil war was over and the sawmill was rebuilt things got back to normal. The school boy pranks along with just plain old forgetfulness was back to being blamed on poor Old Zekial.

It was not long about, 1885 that a drought came along and crops dried up, along with most of the watering holes. Things got about as desperate as they could get for folks so's I reckon more than one good upstanding member of the community took to stealing what they needed and Old Zekial's curse was born to be blamed rather than placing the rightful yet somehow unchristian like, blame on the crisis of drought and its inevitable hunger and stubborn pride.

Don't get me wrong, the folks around these parts prayed for a relief that just wouldn't come. A dry spring gave way to an even drier summer, and the hot dog days of autumn weren't fit even for the dogs. The drought continued on into fall. The first part of that winter was warmer and yes much drier than anyone around these parts could remember.

No doubt about it this was gonna be a sad Christmas. And of course there was only Old Zekial to blame.

The new preacher in town had heard the stories about Zekial Farley. What he had done and what had been done to him. The story didn't set well with him.

He figured that every man, no matter how bad he was, deserved a proper Christian burial.

To the preacher's way of thinking even in death when Christ met out his punishment for us it wasn't because he was giving up on us but it was because he was still working on us. So the preacher took to the pulpit and delivered a sermon that shook the little old ladies to their core, many of whom had prepared the men for battle the day Old Zekial met his end. So began the movement within the community to, at the very least, place a monument for Zekial Farley in The Whispering Springs First Christian Cemetery.

The belief was that in so doing all the bad things happening would come to an end. So the church ladies who didn't ask much of their husbands took to talking up this idea and trying to scrape together pennies and work out barter ideas that would appeal to the local stone mason who wasn't known as a God fearing man.

While the ladies were working to one way of thinking, old Buzz Halfacre was a working to another way of thinking. With the drought and the dismal future ahead of the community his business was a hurting. Now he knew that credit was the one thing the local folk wouldn't ask for; yet was the first thing they'd repay, in one form or another, when it was extended. So it wasn't like the local men hadn't been coming in at all just not as often, and staying for as long.

However, on this night with Christmas just two days away and a stranger a staying in his inn above the tavern; Old Buzz figured the men folk's desperation just might get the best of them. So he started the rumor, or perhaps it was the truth, that the visitor had gold coins. So it was with Christmas looking so sparse, and food pantries a getting so low the local men showed up in droves that night to see this stranger with all the gold.

It's not like this man with gold was a gonna give it away. But, I guess desperation can make a man think illogical thoughts, and respond in illogical ways.

The tavern was full up by an hour past dark and along about 9 maybe 10 that evening moods were a shifting to ugly as the visitor in question started up to his rented room someone grabbed at him, someone else spat words of eternal damnation.

One thing led to another and the poor visitor made it out of the tavern and started running for all he was worth, a few of the younger men present went in pursuit of him. Somehow he made it to that stand of pines and maples not fifty feet from my old back porch.

He was found there the next day when old man Joshua was out a hoping to find some wild honey. It was assumed that he had dropped dead of a heart attack cause, it was reasoned that, if he were killed it didn't take much to do it a cause they wasn't any real marks on his body, least ways not enough to have made him die.

His money was never found, no one in the community turned up with any difference in their lifestyles. And no one in the community left town for over a month a cause on Christmas morning we got hit with a heavy wet snow that pretty much kept people home for the next month.

When I was a growing up the local kids use to go through the woods a twixt here and the tavern turning over rocks just a hoping to find one gold coin.

Truth be told if the stranger really did have gold coins he probably hid them in his rented room amongst his things, in which case old Buzz Halfacre got them.

Anyways the stranger is laid to rest up in the cemetery under a plain brown, pointed rock. The year of his death is the only thing cut into it. No one knew his name or where he was from, least ways not for sure. Any papers he might have had with that information on it old Buzz would have gotten rid of. That way weren't no heirs to be a prying around wanting and expecting to get back whatever old Buzz had managed to take. And it is my belief that he orchestrated the events of the night to take something. Cause one things for sure old Buzz never did nothing that wasn't to his benefit.

Well with the events at the tavern that night and the dead visiting stranger being found the next morning the preacher, the church ladies, and the righteous men of the town took to action and on the first decent day in January that huge marker to Zekial was erected in the cemetery.

Greed's a funny thing you know. It eats people up. Why old Buzz was so greedy his heart was pretty much stone. And his only son, despite being treated no better than a mangy dog by his Pa, turned out to be just like him.

So much like him in fact that when old Buzz died back in 1899 young Buzz stepped in not even closing the tavern for the funeral much less attending it. Truth be told there was no funeral in the real funeral sense for old Buzz. The preacher, who felt it, was his duty, and the coffin maker took old Buzz up to the cemetery and put him in the ground.

I met young Buzz back when I was in my early teens. He was nigh on fifty at the time. Of course I'd always known him to see him. But the time I met him he came right up to the house one night to see my Daddy, and ask him if he'd marry me off to him. Daddy told him he loved me too much to ever let that happen. I was greatly relieved and told my Daddy as much. And Daddy, he told me then and there that if I married it'd be because I loved the man. He also told me that it wouldn't hurt him none at all if I never married. This, in those days and times was a lot for a man to say. He told me that night that all he wanted for me was to be happy in life.

The fact that my Daddy told young Buzz no didn't stop him from finding a Daddy that would say yes. About three months later Buzz married his fourth wife, Henrietta. She was barely 13. As I made mention of before Buzz had married four other wives, none of them lived more than seven years after saying their I do's.

Some of the folks believed he killed them and I suspect that maybe they'd been right. It's for sure that he beat them all. But two years into the marriage, Henrietta became a widow, and I know for a fact that she killed him.

I know this because I was a tending to her back when she lay dying from jaw cancer. She was a pitiful, stinking sight and she had no family, least ways none that cared about her while she lived. Her parents had died long before her, and her brothers what she still had left were scattered to the four corners of the earth, and seeing as how she never bothered to marry a second time she had no children. So since my own family was up and gone from the nest I took it on to myself to tend to Henry, as folks around these parts had taken to calling her long ago.

Before Henry became unable to speak she told me about the things Buzz had done to her and worse the things he had forced her to do to him. Things I'd never heard of, and things I would never repeat. But ever since that spring day back in 1963 that Henry shared these details with me I have always thought that Buzz was no better than Old Zekial and maybe the women in the community should have gathered together and done to Buzz worse than what the men had done to Zekial.

But all that talk and thinking is neither here nor there.

Henry reached her breaking point and started brewing Buzz's morning coffee with rat poison in it. It took a week but on her 16th birthday Henry got the only gift she had wanted, she became a widow. And since Buzz had never managed to have any children, thank the Lord, Henry inherited everything and everything turned out to be quite a lot. But not as much as people might have suspected, she continued to run the tavern up until the depression.

It was long rumored that she could out drink, out smoke, and out cuss any man that came to the tavern. It was also known that she kept law and order in her business with an old hickory club.

When Henrietta closed the tavern she took a bit of her savings and bought the old Hassler farm and took to raising some of the finest quarter horses in the state. Even with the coming of the depression her trading in horses, cattle, and goats made her a profit and kept making her profits right up until three years before she died. That's when she sold off her livestock and retired.

I was with Henry when she passed on in 1963 and in the two years that I tended to her I learned a lot about courage, and bravery. If I ever had a hero it would have to be her. She may not always have been a lady; some proper women might have argued that she wasn't even a proper woman. But she was a survivor. She was willing to do what it took to take care of herself and her needs without sacrificing her true morals. So she drank, so she smoked, so what if she uttered profanities. At least she didn't sell her body, and she wasn't so weak that she saw the need to sell her soul to another marriage.

That sounds as if I'm somehow against marriage. Nothing could be farther from the truth. But I'm an old woman now, and I realize that not every marriage is a good one, and not every man lives up to his promises. I loved my husband, and we were married for close to twenty years. We had five great children, and he let me be who I needed to be. At times I miss him terribly, even though he's been up in that cemetery for nigh on fifty years. But I never remarried, and I am at an age now where I can say that I've been alone longer than I was ever with anyone including my children. And alone ain't so bad, in some ways it is better than being amid a houseful.

There I go off and rambling again. It's just that I learned so much in this town that isn't. And I got all my learning from people that are no longer. Each of those people left behind with me a part of them. I suspect we leave parts of ourselves behind with others so that we, ourselves aren't gone and forgotten. Forgotten like bridges and buildings that get torn down, and towns that get left behind when people move on and technology moves in.

The great depression sure did change things. Who would have ever thought during those trying times that those years were almost the end for this town and these people?

To say that we didn't recognize the depression would be a lie, but to say that it altered things in our community much would also be a lie. Things had always been hard for us. Barter was always the number one currency around here, and we had always been dependant on the weather for our wealth. But we did get newspapers and a few people had a radio, so we were aware of how bad things were for the rest of the world, and we were grateful to our Lord for sparing us the hardest of hardships, for not one man, woman or child was aloud to starve. There was always food to be had if a certain chore got done. And if you were not able to work due to illness, age or injury there were good folk who always stepped up and shared with you what they had. It may not have been cooked the way you liked or even what you liked but it was always enough to ease that burning hunger in your belly.

Like the rest of the nation we prayed for the end to those times that tried the heart and souls of men and women around this nation. And to my way of seeing things we should have thought and been careful what we prayed for. Cause God heard our cries, and watched our lack of quick response to our brothers and sisters overseas. He heard their cries too, and when we were too slow to respond he took the long way to answer our prayers, and allowed a bomb to be dropped on our back porch as it were. When we grabbed a hold of that divine rod and started to fight the good fight, not only did our depression and droughts end once and for all. Our prosperity was increased many times over.

Nothing in this world is ever free; nothing worth having ever comes without a price. This is a truth that I see our children of today losing sight of. This nation paid a price for their prosperity; we lost thousands of men to the war that brought it in. And I think too that we lost a bit too much of our innocence.

The last post mark to go through the Whispering Springs Post Office was December 1947. By 1963, I was an old woman standing next to the grave of my friend Henry. The town shops had all been abandoned, a few of them torn down by then, the school had been closed for eight years. Buses had come along to take our children to the big city school some twenty miles away. I look back and I realize that it was that day that moment in time when I wondered why I hadn't seen the end of the town coming.

Maybe like so many of you, I also had been too caught up in my life to step outside myself and see the meaning behind the changes.

Over the next thirty years I tended to first one neighbor then another. Through their illnesses and deaths I relived more events in this town than I can recall right now. Yet I know that there are more lives, more voices left in me to relay. But the shadows are falling across my porch, and it's time to go in for the evening, eat a bite sleep a bit and then tomorrow..... Well tomorrow I guess I'll pick up this here machine and tell you more about all the lives that were but are no more.

The End